SABOTAGE AT STABLEWAYS

'Look! That isn't a break. The leather's not faulty—it's been deliberately cut!'

'Surely not,' I gasped . . .

A cut stirrup-leather was just one of the puzzling disasters that had lately occurred at Stableways, where Pippa worked as a helper. Obviously someone was trying to discredit the establishment. But who? And why . . .?

As the Boxheath Trials drew near, Pippa and her twin brother Pete worked like mad at their own jumping, while the happenings at the stables became increasingly sinister. Sabotage was one thing, but deliberate attempts to hurt the ponies were even more distressing to Pippa. Also, she seriously began to wonder if Stableways would be able to muster a team to enter at the Trials . . .

Sabotage at Stableways

Judith M. Berrisford

KNIGHT BOOKS
Hodder and Stoughton

For the Dangerfields—Ron, Margaret, Nicholas, Richard and Christopher, with happy memories of when they lived next door.

Copyright © 1982 Judith M. Berrisford

First published by Knight Books 1982

British Library C.I.P.

Berrisford, Judith M.
    Sabotage at Stableways.
    I. Title
    823′.914[J]   PZ7

ISBN 0–340–26812–3

Printed and bound in Great Britain for Hodder and Stoughton Paperbacks, a division of Hodder and Stoughton Ltd., Mill Road, Dunton Green, Sevenoaks, Kent (Editorial Office: 47 Bedford Square, London, WC1 3DP) by Cox & Wyman Ltd, Reading

Contents

1

A horsy disaster

'Carry on, Pippa!'

Gripping my reins more tightly, I urged the grey mare into a canter.

'That's it,' Jenny Harrington called again. 'Increase your pace for the last three strides.'

As I legged Cloud faster, I told myself that I was lucky to have sixteen year-old Jenny as my jumping tutor. She had won a lot of prizes locally and jumping was in her blood. Sam Harrington, her grandfather, who ran Stableways, was ex-army and had been a riding instructor in the Household Cavalry, so he had taught Jenny well.

'One, two, three *up*!' Jenny called the rhythm from beside the jump.

In spite of Jenny's prompting, I still didn't get the timing right. It was my fault, not Cloud's. Left to herself, the mare would no doubt have judged the take-off correctly and cleared the obstacle. As it was, she had to cram in an extra stride. She took off too close, caught the pole with her forelegs and sent it flying.

'Bad luck!' Jenny sympathised as she stooped to replace the bar. 'It was a good try but you haven't quite got the hang of it yet, Pippa.' She ran to mount the young chestnut Arab that she was training for eventing. 'I'll show you again; watch closely while I take Sultan round the course.'

It was impossible not to be thrilled by the effortless ease with which Jenny's fifteen-hand Arab took the jumps. Planks, gate, triple-bar, in-and-out, double oxer and a ditch with rails: Sultan jumped them all faultlessly.

Flaxen tail streaming, the chestnut turned sharply on his quarters in answer to Jenny's barely-perceptible aids. She swung him down the middle of the carefully-constructed course. Ahead of them lay two of the most testing jumps, a hog's-back made of brushwood with a substantial post and rails on either side and, even more difficult, a narrow, quite high, wall.

Jenny cleared the hog's-back perfectly and Sultan gave a pleased swish of his plumed tail as he cantered for the wall. Three strides before take-off, Jenny increased her pace.

Then the disaster happened. As Sultan leapt, Jenny's body seemed to sag to the left. She plummetted from the saddle to pitch sideways against the wooden blocks that made up the 'wall'.

'Oh, Jenny!' I jumped from Cloud and ran to my instructor, who was biting her lip in pain and supporting her left elbow with her right hand. 'You're hurt.'

8

'Yes.' Jenny closed her eyes and I thought she was going to faint, but somehow she managed to pull herself together. 'I'll be all right in a minute.' Her voice wavered but she managed to say: 'Catch Sultan.'

Luckily the chestnut was standing only a few metres away. As I picked up his trailing reins I saw Pete, my twin, getting off a bus in the lane, returning from an athletics practice.

'Thank goodness, you're here!' I called. 'Come quickly.'

Vaulting the gate, my brother ran to Jenny's side. 'What's happened?'

'The stirrup-leather snapped.' Jenny winced. 'And I think I've broken my collar bone.' She managed a wry smile. 'Clever of you to wear a tie today, Pete. It'll make a sling.'

Following Jenny's directions, Pete fastened his tie in a loop round her wrist. Then he knotted the ends on her right shoulder.

'Is it bad?' I asked helplessly.

'Well, it'll have to be X-rayed.' Jenny sighed. 'That means a visit to the hospital.'

As we helped her to her feet, Jenny caught sight of her stirrup-iron lying on the grass.

'I wonder why the leather broke,' she puzzled. 'It was brand new last week. Pippa, get the stirrup-leather from Sultan's saddle for me to see . . . Look! That isn't a break. The leather's not faulty—it's been deliberately cut!'

'Surely not,' I gasped.

'I'm afraid so.' Jenny grimaced as we helped her towards the stable cottage. 'There seems no end to our run of puzzling disasters.'

While we were waiting for the doctor, my thoughts went back to the other disturbing things that had happened at Stableways during the last few weeks. There had been the musty bale of hay that gave Blossom colic. Nobody could understand how it came to be fed to her. Jenny's grandfather always checked every bale on delivery. Then there had been the jumping studs that were stolen from Jenny's tack-bag when she took Sultan to the Riding Club's Trials. It had been a soaking wet day and Jenny had to scratch her entry because she didn't want to risk the Arab falling when the going was so churned up . . . And that wasn't all: there had been the too-tight curb chain on Bogeyman's pelham bridle.

Colonel Lyall, to whom Bogeyman belonged, lived in the big house at Stableways. He had been Sam Harrington's Commanding Officer and when they both retired from the Army the Colonel had leased the stables, head groom's cottage and twenty-four hectares of pasture to Jenny's grandfather. Jenny and her grandfather were dependent on him to allow them to carry on running the stables. That was why the trouble with the curb chain had seemed so serious.

A link had been missing from the chain so that the bit had pinched Bogeyman's mouth. It had made him play up in the midst of the traffic when Colonel

Lyall took him to be shod. The Colonel and Bogeyman had nearly been run down by a juggernaut lorry. It had made the Colonel wonder whether the traffic round Dormhill was becoming too dangerous for riding, and whether it was safe to allow the stables to carry on.

Sergeant Sam, as Jenny's grandfather was affectionately known, had then promised the Colonel never to allow any riders to leave Stableways unaccompanied, and to ensure that any riders crossing the bypass to reach the heath always used the subway. Even so, we knew that the safety factor was uppermost in the Colonel's mind. There was always the risk that any mishap, such as Jenny's, might cause him to reconsider and close down Stableways—the only riding stables in the urban sprawl of Dormhill.

'The doctor's on his way.' Pete's voice from the telephone broke into my thoughts. He turned to Jenny. 'I dare say he'll be able to take you in his car for the X-ray. Pippa and I will have to hold the fort here until your grandfather comes back from the horse sale.'

The kettle whistled. A moment later, as I stirred the sugar into Jenny's tea, we saw a tall shadow fall across the kitchen window.

'Colonel Lyall!' Jenny groaned. 'What's he going to make of this latest "accident"?'

'He'll be sympathetic, of course,' I tried to console her.

'Yes, I know, but this might well make him decide not to renew Grandpa's lease.'

I sighed, knowing Jenny could be right. This latest misfortune might be the deciding factor in Stableways' fate. Jenny's grandfather was getting old. The Colonel might feel that his not having noticed the faulty stirrup leather showed that he was losing his grip. Colonel Lyall might decide to sell Stableways. The big house could easily be converted into flats and the grazing land become a housing estate.

The Colonel would be able to afford to buy Sergeant Sam an annuity to help out his Army pension. But how could Sergeant Sam and Jenny live happily without horses around them?

And where would the pony-mad children of Dormhill ride if Stableways was no more?

2

Enter gypsy Benny

'So you two children had to cope alone,' the Colonel said, after the doctor had driven Jenny to hospital for an X-ray. 'Where's Sergeant Sam?'

'He had to go to the horse sale,' Pete explained. 'He's looking out for another jumping pony.'

'Then he ought to have asked me to come over to take charge,' said the Colonel. 'He's too independent by far about asking favours. This settles it: in future when he's away from the stables he must leave a grown-up in charge. The so-called stableman's too young and irresponsible to fit the bill. Where is he?'

'Ernie persuaded Jenny to let him go early,' I said. 'He told her he wanted to ride down to Brighton on his motor-bike for the opening of the new disco.'

The Colonel glared impatiently at his watch. 'I'm due in town for a Regimental reunion at eight. I intended to catch the seven-five train, but I'll now have to phone my apologies and stay to give you a hand with evening stables.'

'Oh, there's no need for that, Colonel Lyall,' I

said quickly, glancing at my brother. 'Pete and I can manage.'

Colonel Lyall looked at us, still doubtful. 'Well, all the horses are quiet, and you're both used to the routine. I suppose you might cope on your own for once, though I don't like to leave you to it, particularly after all I've been saying about the need for a grown-up to be in charge.'

Pete met his gaze directly. 'Don't worry, sir. You'll miss the chance of seeing all your old friends if you don't go to the reunion. Honestly, Pippa and I can manage, and Sergeant Sam will soon be back.'

The Colonel still hesitated. Then he said at last: 'Very well. As you say, I can't let down the Regiment.'

*   *   *   *

'Just my bad luck,' Pete grumbled as we humped fresh straw to deepen Sultan's bedding for the night. 'I'm due at the Athletics Club at seven. Now I'll be held up here for goodness knows how long.'

'You volunteered,' I reminded him. 'Besides, there's more to life than athletics.'

'Hoof and hide, I suppose,' Pete sighed. 'When I agreed to come to Stableways with you, Pippa, I didn't bargain for it becoming a full-time occupation.'

'You like it well enough when you're riding.' Giving Sultan an extra heavy pat on the quarters in my exasperation, I followed Pete out of the loose-box. 'It's when it comes to mucking-out and tack-cleaning that you start to moan. Anyway—' I headed for the fodder room '—go to your precious running track.'

'Serve you right if I did,' said Pete, 'but you know I've got to stay. I promised the Colonel.'

At that moment there came a clatter of hooves on the cobbles and, before we could collect our wits, Sultan cantered past us heading for the open gate of the field.

'You can't have tied him properly,' Pete accused me.

'But I did,' I protested. Then I remembered. I had sometimes seen Sultan tugging at the head-rope with his teeth when Jenny had left him tied up. Arabs were clever and Sultan had persisted until at last he had managed to pull the slip-knot free. 'Well, he's loose now,' I groaned, realising that to argue any further with Pete wouldn't help matters. 'And he's not always easy to catch. Wait here while I fetch some pony-nuts.'

If Pete had waited as I'd told him, all might have been well, but he was too much a boy of action to be thwarted by the whim of a horse. When I came back with the pony-nuts, I was just in time to see Sultan break from the corner into which Pete had driven him. The Arab charged. Pete fell backwards amid the buttercups and Sultan, with a defiant swish of his tail, rose at the fence into the next field.

Sultan cleared the solid wooden railings with ease, but he put a foot into a muddy patch on landing, stumbled and slipped into the ditch which was swollen following the recent bad weather.

The wet ground of the bank crumbled under Sultan's forefeet as he struggled to lever himself out. Thoroughly frightened now, he began to thresh about.

'Steady, boy.' I tried to keep my voice calm as we climbed over the fence to help.

Sultan's struggles had now thickened the water with mud. His eyes were rolling and his nostrils flared crimson. He was so terrified at his predicament that we found it difficult to get near enough to help.

'Quiet, Sultan,' Pete urged, trying to reach for his halter. Sultan tossed his head as he made yet another despairing lunge at the bank. Then he tried to rear. This time he overbalanced and rolled sideways into the ditch.

Now he was in danger of drowning.

'We've got to keep his head up.' Peter plunged in beside the horse. 'Quickly, Pippa! Fetch help.'

At that moment there came a shout from across the fields and a gypsy-looking boy wriggled through the thorn-hedge and ran across the field towards us.

'Watch out!' he called to Pete. 'Stand clear, or the horse will roll on you. Let me get to him.'

The boy splashed into the ditch between Pete and the fear-crazed Arab.

'Whoa, there! Steady, fellow! Let's be having you.' In a crooning whisper the boy talked to Sultan. His hands supported the Arab's head and he blew soothingly into the dilated nostrils.

I knew the boy by sight. He was known as gypsy Benny and he lived in a caravan, near the Corporation rubbish tip, with his mother and his stepfather. We'd sometimes seen Benny hanging around the stables. Sergeant Sam had usually chased him off. He had once been in trouble with the police for stealing food from the supermarket for his lurcher bitch. He'd been let off but he'd been taken into care for a while, in a Council Home, because his mother had to go into hospital for an operation. Benny's real father, who'd been drowned while poaching salmon, had been a gypsy horse-trader, known as Rutland Reuben.

It seemed that Benny had inherited his father's Romany skill of horse-whispering.

The Arab was becoming calmer. He was no longer threshing and seemed to be listening to Benny's quiet coaxing.

'That's it,' the boy encouraged Sultan. 'Roll over, fellow. Bring your feet under you.'

Pete and I gazed in surprise as the Arab responded.

Now that he had all four feet on the bottom of the ditch Sultan was able to raise his body clear of the water. He was trembling and shaken, yet calm.

'Help me on to his back.' Benny turned to Pete. 'I'll ride him to the culvert. There's firm ground there. If he can get his forefeet on to that, he may be able to drag himself out.'

At the culvert Benny sprang on to the bank. He grasped Sultan's halter and I tugged at his canvas head-collar. We pulled hard, encouraging the horse to heave himself clear. Meanwhile Pete shoved at his quarters. With a lot of scrabbling and a final effort that flung lumps of mud into Pete's face and hair, the Arab struggled on to firm ground.

'That's it, boy.' Benny put an arm over Sultan's neck as he crooned fondly to the horse.

Sultan lowered his head and the boy began to stroke his ears with an upwards movement. 'This'll warm him,' he explained. 'Now we'll get him into a stable and I'll dry him off for you.'

Benny was still working on Sultan, wisping his coat to bring up a body-glow, when Sergeant Sam returned at half-past eight. Pete and I had watered and fed the ponies that lived out in the field. Now we were in Sultan's loose-box, handing Benny fresh straw and standing by to rug up the Arab.

'Anybody around?' Sergeant Sam's voice sounded above the slam of the estate car door. He blinked when he saw Pete and me. 'What's this then?'

'Jenny fell off Sultan—' I began, trying to break the bad news gently.

Sergeant Sam nodded briskly. 'I know. I was on my way back here when I saw her being driven off by the doctor, so I did a U-turn. I've been with her at the hospital. Everything's under control.' He looked again at Benny. 'What's he doing here?'

Benny moved his feet shiftily.

'I know you said you didn't want me here, hanging round your horses, mister,' said Benny, 'but this one was in trouble and I had to help.'

'That's right,' Pete explained what had happened. 'Sultan might have been drowned if it hadn't been for Benny.'

'Hmm! Able to smell horse-trouble from a mile off—just like his dad, I reckon. Well, maybe I've misjudged him.' Sergeant Sam turned to Benny. 'Seeing as you can't keep away from horses you can come to the stables now and then and lend a hand. We'll be short of helpers now Jenny's hurt.'

'Thank you, mister.' Benny's eyes shone.

Sergeant Sam gave him a hard stare. 'Well, listen to me, lad. You're a horse-whisperer, same as your dad, and, in my experience, gypsy horse-whisperers have a way of making horses "walk"—' He looked stern. 'There's to be none of that—and I don't want other people's belongings to go "walking" either. You can help here as long as you behave yourself. Is that clear?' He glanced from Pete to me. 'I may live to regret this, and goodness knows what the Colonel will say about me giving Benny the freedom of the place, but I suppose I owe it to the lad for saving Sultan.'

'You won't regret it, Mr Harrington,' I said rashly.

Then, unseen by Sergeant Sam, Benny gave me a conspiratorial wink as though he was thanking me for being on the side of a gypsy.

Oh, dear! I thought, remembering Benny's reputation. Could he really be trusted?

3

Who will ride Sultan?

'I didn't tell Grandpa about the stirrup-leather,'
Jenny, back from the hospital, confided to Pete and
I when we were helping her to put out the feeds the
following morning. 'I wanted him to see the
deliberate cut for himself. Otherwise he'd never
believe that anyone would do anything so wicked.'
She glanced up at us. 'Where did you put the
leather?'

I looked blank and Pete shook his head. 'I suppose
in all the panic we didn't bother to pick it up, but I
think I know where it'll be.'

Five minutes later he came back from the field
empty-handed. 'It's gone!' he reported.

'Someone else must have taken it,' I said.

'Yes,' groaned Jenny, awkwardly grabbing the
scoop with one hand, determined to work despite
her injury. 'Perhaps the person who cut it decided to
do away with the evidence.'

'We can't be sure of that,' Pete said. 'Your
grandfather or even the Colonel, may have gone to

the field to see where you fell, and then picked up the leather. It's probably on the tack-room bench.'

Jenny handed me the scoop. 'You and Pete carry on putting out the feeds. I'm going to the tack-room to look.'

When Pete and I joined her there to report that the feed buckets were ready, Jenny told us that she had yet again drawn a blank. 'It's a mystery where that leather's gone to, but I'm not going to ask Grandpa or Colonel Lyall and upset them. Grandpa has quite enough on his mind now I'm out of action. He's got to find another rider for Sultan: he's come on too well not to be entered in the Boxheath Trials.'

'Who'll ride him, then?' I asked.

'There are two possibilities,' Jenny told us. 'With Grandpa to give them extra coaching, there's no reason why either Ian Hamilton or Colin Blackmoor shouldn't compete.'

I looked thoughtful. 'Ian's not as polished as Colin at dressage,' I said, 'but he'd do better than Colin in the cross-country. He's got more nerve.'

I hoped that Ian would be chosen. He had a natural way with animals, comforting and reassuring. Horses, dogs and cats knew where they were with him. He seemed to have his vet father's knack of making a sick or frightened animal feel secure. Colin on the other hand, was quick and rash, but his nerve did not always live up to his showy approach. His heart wasn't always 'on the other side of the jump', as Sergeant Sam would have said. Yet Colin was brilliant at dressage, polished and patient.

Perhaps it was the showmanship that he had inherited from his actress mother that enabled him to give such a confident, sometimes conceited performance.

'It's going to be hard for your grandfather to choose between them,' I said now, 'but I'm sure he'll make the right decision.'

Jenny nodded. 'Grandpa's got both boys coming up to the stables this afternoon. He wants to see how Sultan will react—'

She broke off as heavy footsteps sounded on the cobbles and Ernie Topsall, Sergeant Sam's stable-man came past.

'Buck up with those feeds, you two,' Ernie called to Pete and me. 'There's a jumping class at half-past ten, and we don't want any of the gees going down with colic because they haven't had time to digest their food.'

'Right-ho, Ernie,' Pete called cheerfully.

'Don't mind Ernie,' Jenny said when he was out of earshot. 'He gets a bit edgy at times.' She paused, and her brow knitted. 'For some reason he seems rather thick with Colin. That's why I didn't want him to hear what I was telling you. It might make him resent Ian if he thought he was the rider that I'd prefer for Sultan.'

'Ernie and Colin.' I puzzled. 'They seem an unlikely pair of friends. What have they really got in common?'

Pete shrugged. 'Well I suppose motor-bikes make the whole world kin. Colin will be seventeen next week and he says his father has promised him a Suzuki.'

'Mr Blackmoor seems to have more money than sense,' Jenny said. 'I would have thought a boy like Colin needed a motor-scooter, or something of that sort, before he went on to a powerful bike. He's too hot-headed by far.'

'Well, at least, he's had plenty of practical experience,' Pete pointed out. 'For some months now he's been riding Ernie's Kawasaki round the old air-field.'

'Fancy that!' I raised my eyebrows. 'The things you learn about people. Who'd have thought Colin would bother with motor-bikes when he's the pick of these horses to ride?'

'I don't think Colin is all that keen on horses.' Jenny said shrewdly. 'He likes the figure he cuts, and the sound of applause, which is yet another reason why I'd prefer Grandpa to choose Ian to ride Sultan at Boxheath.'

*   *   *   *

Several of the pupils stayed on after their rides that afternoon to see the cross-country and dressage tests that Sergeant Sam had arranged for the two boys. The Colonel forsook his usual afternoon nap to be present, and young Benny just 'happened' to be passing. Drawn like a magnet by anything to do with horses, he watched agog as Ian and Colin walked the course.

23

Ian was first to ride over the short cross-country course. We could see that Jenny's Arab recognised him as a firm friend. When Ian fondled his head and spoke affectionately to him before mounting, Sultan flickered one of his elegant ears in recognition. Then when Ian mounted, the horse bent his neck and plumed his tail proudly. This was a rider whom he could trust and for whom he would do his best.

As we had expected, the cross-country course held no terrors for Ian. He rode boldly, realising that Sultan was young and inexperienced, and knowing that it was up to him as rider to make the decisions, set the pace, use the necessary impulsion and judge the right spot to take off for each jump.

Pete ran after them for the first few fences to see how Sultan fared.

'Ian's in fine form,' he reported when he panted back to us after the fifth fence. 'Sultan's going just as well for him as he does for Jenny.'

'I should say he is.' The Colonel spoke from under his binoculars. 'They're just coming to the water now,' he reported. 'They're taking it. They're over. Oh, good boy!'

Breathlessly we waited until horse and rider reappeared approaching the hog's-back, the last but one of the homeward jumps. Sultan was going great guns now. Ian was galloping him as if he was riding against the clock. Thud-thud-*thud!* He increased his speed for the take-off. Up and over! The chestnut Arab soared. We saw him land clear; then, with a characteristic flick of his tail, he was off again, flat out for the wall, the final jump.

'Well done, my boy.' The Colonel was first with his congratulations as Ian reined up after a triumphant ride.

'That'll take a bit of beating, Colin.' I heard Ernie say.

Colin Blackmoor bit his lip. He crammed his crash cap hard down over his sleek dark hair. Then, flicking his switch against his booted leg—a habit he had when sullen—he strode to take over the horse.

'I'll give Sultan a bit of a breather,' he said to Sergeant Sam, and I noticed that he was standing hesitantly beside the Arab's head as if putting off the moment when he would have to jump.

'Off you go then.' Sergeant Sam had a finger on the button of his stop-watch. 'Don't go too slowly. It's not a time competition but I'd like to see how you shape against the clock.'

Colin swung a leg over Sultan's saddle. Tense-faced he shortened his reins. Then they were off!

This time Pete did not race behind. Instead he stood with Jenny and I beside the Colonel.

'He's doing well so far,' Colonel Lyall remarked. 'He's over the in-and-out without any problems. Now he's on the bank. Oh, he doesn't like the look of the post-and-rails. I expect he's worrying in case Sultan jumps too big and flies the bank on the other side. Bad luck! The pole's down. Now he's muffing the descent. Sorry, Sam, I wonder after all if this particular protégé of yours will make the grade?'

'I wouldn't say that, sir.' Sergeant Sam was reserving judgment. 'Anyone can have an off-day.'

'Fair enough, Sam,' conceded the Colonel. 'Let's see how Colin shapes over the rest of the course. Then there's the dressage test to be considered. Yes, by all means wait until the end of the afternoon before you make up your mind which boy is the better all-rounder.'

4

What a dirty trick!

Everybody's gaze was on Colin and Sultan as they came into view from behind the copse.

Colin now seemed to have recovered his nerve. He was pushing Sultan faster as they approached the hog's-back.

The Arab had his mind on the finish and whatever fuss and reward might be forthcoming. Taking over the initiative from his rider, he snatched at his bit, poked out his nose and galloped hard.

'He's coming at the jump too fast,' sighed the Colonel.

'It looks as if Colin's riding for a fall,' Pete prophesied at my side.

Although, like most of the other watchers, I wanted Ian to be the boy whom Sergeant Sam would choose to ride Sultan, I hoped that the Arab would not come down. I crossed my fingers as he took the jump too fast. Luckily, however, Sultan's stretch was enough to take him over even such a wide spread at his now break-neck pace.

I breathed again as, with his usual whisk of the

tail, Sultan collected himself and galloped for the wall.

But the Arab was still going far too fast. We saw Colin take a pull on the reins to try to steady him. This unbalanced Sultan. He put in an extra stride and took off too close to the wall.

The Arab rose steeply, all four legs tucked well under him. But, he was too near to the obstacle and he knocked off the top two rows of wooden bricks. I saw Colin's mouth twitch in petulance. Then the showman in him enabled him to regain his composure.

'Not one of my best days,' he announced as he reined up before Sergeant Sam and the Colonel.

'Hard luck, mate.' Ernie came forward to take Sultan's reins. 'Tell you what,' he suggested, turning to Sergeant Sam, 'why not let Colin, here, carry straight on with the dressage? That ought to show what he's made of, eh?'

Colin opened his mouth to protest then fell silent and I thought I saw Ernie give him the shadow of a wink.

'I think Sultan should have a breather,' said Jenny.

'Not necessary,' put in the Colonel. 'A couple of short rounds oughtn't to be too much for a horse like Sultan.' He glanced at Jenny's grandfather—'Carry on, Corporal of Horse. Let's see how the lad shapes at the dressage test, if he's game.'

'Oh, I'm game enough, sir.' Colin transferred his

reins to his left hand while he dropped his right stirrup-leather a couple of holes.

Aided by Ernie he adjusted his other leather, straightened his cap and walked Sultan on a loose rein to the dressage arena, which was already marked out.

'Good boy, that!' remarked the Colonel, watching Colin's straight back, relaxed hands and the way he kept his gaze straight ahead. 'Rides long—true Household Cavalry style. Got good manners too. I wouldn't have minded having him as one of my own young officers.'

I caught Pete's eye and groaned. There was no doubt who would be the Colonel's choice to ride the Arab at Boxheath—Colin!

Looking straight in front of him, Colin walked Sultan in a large circle, collected him firmly and entered the arena by the large letter 'A' which Sergeant Sam had pasted on to a cardboard display card.

Moving in a straight line, Colin walked Sultan forward until he was directly opposite Sergeant Sam and the Colonel. He halted centre, gave a little bow and a formal smile to the 'judges', then tracked right at an extended trot. Sultan's dressage movements were so graceful they almost took my breath away. The Arab seemed to be trotting on air. Head flexed, cat-like ears forward, flaxen tail plumed, he moved as if on a cloud. He made me think of Pegasus, the mythical winged horse.

Colin changed reins. Sultan's change of leg at the

trot was faultless. Pete and I knew it to be the result of Jenny's and her grandfather's patient schooling, but to the Colonel it must have looked an impressive part of Colin's performance. His riding in the dressage test was impossible to fault.

He cantered a controlled circle, brought Sultan back to the trot and executed the turns on the forehand correctly. Sultan moved fluidly and well in the free walk, without a single jog and all the time Colin sat apparently motionless, his aids imperceptible except to the trained eye. I knew what the Colonel meant. As Colin rode, straight-legged, body erect, face expressionless, it was possible to imagine him in the plumed helmet, glinting breast-plate and scarlet tunic of the Household Cavalry.

Colin led off directly at the letter 'C' for the second canter and came back accurately to the trot as he passed the letter again. Now he needed only to walk up the centre and make his final bow, but instead he put in an extra exercise of his own. Smoothly and competently he trotted a serpentine, reversed and serpentined again in the other direction.

'Well done, boy.' Even Sergeant Sam was impressed. He congratulated Colin as he brought Sultan back to the watching group.

'Better let the horse have a breather now.' Grasping Sultan's reins, Ernie took charge as Colin slid to the ground.

Gypsy Benny ran forward, eager to help take off the Arab's saddle.

30

'Get out of the way with you.' Ernie shooed Benny away from the Arab's shifting feet.

Unabashed, Benny slipped a grimy hand in his pocket and brought out a grey-looking peppermint. 'All the best horses like mints,' he said, dodging Ernie's threatened cuff and offering the sweet to Sultan with a cheeky grin. 'Even Red Rum has 'em, according to the telly.'

Ten minutes later it was Ian's turn to go through the dressage test. Picking up the saddle before Ernie could intervene, he slid it gently into position on the Arab's back.

Sultan shifted restlessly and I noticed a twitch ripple the chestnut silk of his withers. Ian raised the saddle a fraction and carefully smoothed the horse's hairs.

As soon as Ian was in the saddle the Arab began to jog.

'Oh, dear,' sighed Pete. 'That doesn't look good for the dressage test. Sultan is too fresh. That ten-minute break seems to have been a mistake.'

To my surprise and dismay, the Arab did not seem to settle down with Ian as he had with Colin. He moved crab-wise into the arena and, when Ian brought him to a halt in front of Sergeant Sam and the Colonel, he was not standing straight. As Ian walked him on, Sultan began to jog again. Then he brought his head almost down to his knees and tossed it up again.

'It looks almost as if something's irritating him,' I said to Pete.

Overhearing, Ernie poured scorn on the idea. 'The horse's just fidgety, that's all.' He turned to Sergeant Sam. 'If you notice, Mr Harrington, young Ian doesn't keep his hands still enough. And look at those legs. Niggling and nudging the horse he is, most of the time. That's what's making the Arab restless.'

'Ian's not in the same category as Colin when it comes to dressage,' the Colonel said when Sultan muffed a turn on the quarters, jibbed at being asked to rein back and bucked his way into the second canter. 'The boy's no finesse. Plenty of dash and courage when it comes to jumping, but too heavy-handed altogether in the dressage arena.'

'It's not Ian's fault.' Jenny loyally came to the defence of her friend. 'There's something wrong with Sultan. He doesn't usually behave like this.'

'He may not behave like that with you, Miss Jenny,' Ernie put in, 'but then you've got hands like velvet. It's young Ian's handling that's upset the Arab.'

As though he found the bickering tiresome, the Colonel grunted and then looked pointedly at his watch.

'Come on, Sam.' He turned to the Sergeant. 'If we're going to have a look at the mare that's for sale at Boxheath, we'd better go now. It's gone half-past three.'

No sooner were the Colonel and Sergeant Sam off the scene than Sultan began to play up again. He kicked up his heels and then reared, taking Ian off his guard and almost making him drop the reins.

Before any of us had a chance to do anything, Benny ran forward. Reaching up past Ian he caught at Sultan's bridle as the Arab pawed the air, snorting.

'Come on, fellow. What's wrong?' Bringing Sultan down he laid a soothing hand on the chestnut's neck.

The Arab twitched away, quivering the skin of his withers.

'Something's irritating him.' Jenny moved forward to look but Sultan shied away.

'Best leave him to me, miss.' Dropping his voice to a low croon, Benny yet again practised the ancient art of the horse-whisperer. 'There, fellow. Quiet, boy. Let me see.'

He ran his hands over Sultan's withers, parting the hair and fingering the skin. He turned to Jenny. 'I can feel something powdery.' He withdrew his hand and sniffed at his fingers before holding them out to Pete. 'What does that smell like?'

'Itching powder!' Pete exclaimed. 'What a dirty trick!'

5

A threatening letter

Jenny looked horrified. 'Who could have done such a dreadful thing?'

'None of us.' Colin was quick to say. 'Not even Benny. This is the kind of mindless trick a non-horsy person would play. Some yobbo must have come wandering round, got into the tack room and dusted the itching powder under the saddle. It must have worked into the hair of Sultan's withers when the saddle was put on.'

My twin looked at Colin. 'What motive could anyone have for doing such a nasty thing?'

'The same motive they would have had for feeding mouldy hay to Sultan, or cutting Jenny's stirrup-leather,' Colin said blandly. 'To make Stableways look inefficiently run, of course.'

'You could be right about the mouldy hay and the stirrup-leather,' I said slowly, 'but I don't agree about the motive for the itching powder. Whoever put it under Sultan's saddle had something to gain by ruining Ian's dressage test.'

'What do you mean?' Colin blustered. 'I admit it

would be great if Sergeant Sam chose me to ride the Arab at Boxheath, but I certainly wouldn't have any part in such a dirty trick as dusting Sultan's saddle with itching powder in order to spoil Ian's chances.'

'Perhaps not.' I had to agree. 'But someone else might.' I remembered the look I had seen Ernie give Colin when he suggested that Sultan should have a breather before changing riders. It had been Ernie who had removed the Arab's saddle and wisped him down ... 'Ernie's a friend of yours,' I challenged rashly. 'It could have been him.'

'As if I'd do such a thing.' Ernie reacted with quick indignation. 'You want to keep your suspicions to yourself, miss, and not go slandering people that the stable depends on. How do you think this place would keep going if it wasn't for me? With Jenny crocked and Mr Harrington getting no younger, there has to be someone young and strong to do the heavy work. What would Mr Harrington say if I were to walk out because of you, eh? A few pony-mad kid helpers wouldn't save Stableways then.'

'Calm down, Ernie.' Pete turned his head to give me a warning look. 'Sometimes my sister speaks without thinking what she's saying.'

'That's right.' Ian backed him up, realising it was necessary to soothe Ernie. 'Some outsider's been playing tricks. From now on we must all keep a keen look-out for strangers around the stables.'

I don't think any of us were really convinced by the 'stranger' theory, but we all resolved to be on

35

our guard to prevent anything else going wrong at Stableways.

It wasn't possible to keep an eye on everything all the time, of course, especially as there were so many jobs to do. Before we went home for supper that evening every piece of saddlery and every bridle had to be taken to pieces, wiped over and inspected before being put away in the right order ready for the next day.

Most of the ponies were kept at grass. They worked hard and needed extra food. So there were hay-nets and pony-nuts to be distributed. Then we had to see that the water troughs were clean and that the water pipes which fed them were trickling freely. We had to make sure that there was a salt lick in each field.

The bigger animals, the show ponies, and the grown-ups' hacks and hunters lived in loose-boxes. They had to be watered and fed. All stable dirt had to be removed from the loose-boxes and a thick layer of straw spread for the night. As it was Easter, it was still cold at night, so the stable inmates wore rugs which had to be brushed and aired each day. Not for nothing had Sergeant Sam been Corporal of Horse. Usually the standard of equipment, grooming and the fitness of horses and ponies would have passed the scrutiny of the keenest inspection.

That night I was so tired I fell asleep almost as soon as I snuggled under the duvet. Mummy let me sleep on the next morning and, by the time I eventually went downstairs, Daddy had left on his day's selling trip and Pete had gone down to the Athletics Club for hurdling practice.

Mummy was grilling bacon when the postman came, so I ran through into the hall to pick up the letters. Good, there was one for me! I thought it might be from a school friend on holiday, or perhaps even an invitation to a party.

It wasn't until I drew out an untidy sheet of ruled paper, with a message written in badly-formed capitals, that I realised there was anything odd about it.

WATCH OUT, PIPPA. DON'T MEDDLE WITH WHAT IS NOT YOUR BUSINESS. IF YOU DO, YOU WILL BE OUT OF STABLEWAYS FOR EVER.

There was no signature.

Shocked, I stared at the anonymous letter. I wanted to be rid of the horrible thing. Impulsively I screwed it up and threw it into the newly-lit fire in the grate.

Immediately I knew I'd done the wrong thing. I ought to have kept it and showed it to Daddy. He'd have known what to do. Now I'd destroyed the evidence. What a fool I was! I couldn't even remember exactly what the letter said, not word for word. Anyway, it didn't make sense. What meddling had I been doing?

But somebody must have thought I'd seen something suspicious . . . some guilty person sneaking out of the tack-room after Jenny's stirrup-leather was cut, for instance ... or some gloved hand rubbing the itching powder into Sultan's coat?

One thing was clear. Someone meant me harm—just as someone had intended to injure Jenny by cutting the stirrup-leather.

As I looked out of the window a cloud came over the sun and I shivered.

*   *   *   *

'You were a clot to burn that letter,' Pete pointed out as we made our way along the suburban avenues to the stables later that morning. 'There might have been fingerprints on it. Or a hand-writing expert could have found out who wrote it. The police might have found the guilty person in a few hours. Now we can only guess.'

'It was Ernie, of course!' I decided. 'And he was responsible for the itching powder, too. The letter completely disproves the mindless yobbo theory.'

'It sounds possible,' Pete admitted thoughtfully. 'After all Sultan went well enough in Colin's dressage test. There was no sign of itching then.'

'He started to fidget as soon as Ian mounted,' I recalled.

'And there was certainly a break between Colin's dressage and Ian's,' said Pete. He screwed up his eyes trying to recall the details. 'Yes, it was Ernie who suggested the break. You're right there, Pippa.'

I nodded. 'That's when Ernie must have rubbed the itching powder into Sultan's coat, when he was wisping him. Do you think Colin was in on it too, Pete?'

My twin looked grim. 'They could be a couple of real villains and clever with it. That's why we've got to be rather clever, too, Pippa, and not go round making accusations until we've found some real proof.'

I felt uneasy. 'We'll just have to keep our wits about us and try to carry on as though I've not been threatened. Oh, Pete, I'm scared!'

*   *   *   *

By the time we reached the stables, the morning ride, with Sergeant Sam in charge, had already left for the heath.

'Never mind,' said Jenny. 'I've got other plans for you two. I want you to get in some jumping practice. Stableways needs to do well in this season's shows if we're to stay in business. John Gregg will ride Soldier, Billy Lane's riding Turpin and I've entered Amanda Howe on Nibbles for the under-sixteen trials. But there are ordinary jumping competitions, too, and I thought of entering you for the Junior Pairs. You'll have to work hard, of course but, with the usual bond between twins, you ought to do better than most when it comes to keeping together.'

Pete and I exchanged glances. Would we really be any good? We needed a lot of practice. Of course, the jumps would not be very high for the Junior Pairs, and Cloud and Cavalier were two able jumpers. Pete and I would have to take the jumps side by side. We would have to keep together all the way round the course: there would be penalties if either one of us dropped behind.

'We'll have a go!' Pete impulsively decided for us both.

We caught the ponies and were on our way to the stable-yard to tack-up when a small black-and-white smooth-haired terrier pup, with one brown ear and a brown patch over one eye, ran from the back door of the Colonel's house and dashed around us, yapping. Cloud took no notice but Cavalier was more excitable. The terrier's yapping made him shy, leaving Pete at the end of his reins, tugging to get him under control.

'Here, Rags!' A small girl, blonde pony-tail bobbing behind her yellow jersey, ran across the yard after the pup, 'Bad dog!'

Oblivious to his young mistress's command, the terrier pup darted at Cavalier's heels.

'Call your dog off,' Pete warned, 'or he might get kicked.'

'Best put him under lock and key, Miss Emma.'

Ernie Topsall put down the shafts of the barrow which he had been pushing and came across to intervene. 'Kids!' he snorted with an impatient grimace in Emma's direction. 'Colonel Lyall's granddaughter—pony-mad like the rest of you, and even more of a nuisance. Here!' He dived to scoop up the wriggling Rags and removed him from the danger zone of Cavalier's heels.

'Give him to me, Ernie,' Emma held out her arms. 'He doesn't like strangers. He might bite you.'

'Yeh? Him and who else?' Ernie held the writhing terrier high above his head.

'Put him down.' Emma was almost in tears.

'Not until he's learned a few manners.' Ernie tucked the little dog tightly under his arm and administered a reproving tap to his muzzle.

'Grrr!'—the puppy gave a baby growl and tried to snap at Ernie's fingers. In response Ernie put a ham-like hand over the pup's nose and held his mouth tightly shut.

'Beast!' Emma hurled herself at Ernie who again swung the puppy up out of reach.

Just then Ian came out of Sultan's loose-box.

'What's going on?' His quick glance took in the situation. 'Turn it up, Ernie! Give Emma back her puppy.'

'Who's going to make me?' Ernie demanded, holding the still-wriggling Rags high in the air.

'I am,' Ian said, advancing on the youth.

Just then, the Colonel's estate car turned into the yard and Ernie quickly handed the puppy to Emma.

'What's this? A union meeting?' The Colonel asked as he got out of the car. His gaze stopped at Ernie. 'Haven't you any work to do, Topsall?'

'Yes sir, I have,' Ernie was unabashed. 'But I don't see how I can carry on with it unless that pup of Miss Emma's is shut in where it can't do any harm. Nipping at Cavalier's heels, he was—might have had his head kicked in if I hadn't come on the scene.'

The Colonel turned to Jenny. 'Is that right?'

'Well, yes—' Jenny hesitated.

'Then that's settled,' the Colonel said briskly. 'Emma, take Rags indoors, and don't let him anywhere near the stables except on a leash. Topsall's got quite enough to do without you making his job more difficult.'

6

A real baddie

For the next few days Pete and I worked hard at our jumping.

Jenny started us over poles. Then we moved on to cavaletti, fixed knife-rest-like jumps which could be turned over to vary the height.

I found it easier jumping side by side with Pete than alone. Pete seemed unerringly able to judge the right spot for take-off and he had a natural instinct for pace. Pounding along beside him, I only had to match Cloud's strides to those of Cavalier.

'You're coming on well, both of you,' Jenny enthused at the end of our first week of practice. 'Keep it up, and you won't disgrace us at Boxheath.'

Whenever Pete and I were jumping, Emma watched longingly, her terrier, Rags, on a lead. Sergeant Sam had allotted Emma an eleven-hand Exmoor, Pixie, to ride. Past the first wildness of her youth, mealy-nosed Pixie was now a safe pony for a child. Sam Harrington was not going to take any risks with the Colonel's granddaughter.

'I can ride very well really,' Emma insisted as she

43

followed Pete and me to the field. 'We often jump small fences at school. I think Jenny's mean not to let me try.'

'I heard that, Emma.' Jenny turned back with a smile. 'If you like you can fasten up Rags in the house and saddle Pixie.'

'Are you going to let me jump?' Emma's eyes sparkled.

'Well, we'll see how you get on,' Jenny said. 'To begin with you can trot Pixie up and down the jumping lane over poles on the ground.'

Emma pulled a face. 'I don't think much of that,' she said.

'Well, it's that or nothing,' Jenny said.

'Cheer up, Emma,' I encouraged. 'Poles on the ground are better than sulking.'

'We all have to start somewhere.' Pete gave her blonde pony-tail a playful tweak. 'Even the famous jumping stars on television started over poles on the ground.'

'Very well then,' agreed Emma.

Pete and I had our jumping practice interrupted several times that afternoon as Emma kept calling to Jenny to watch her trot Pixie over the poles. Presently she let Emma canter down the jumping lane. Then, buckling a strap round the Exmoor's neck, she raised each of the poles to a foot.

'Let's see you try those.' Jenny smiled encouragingly at Emma. 'You've got a firm seat and good hands. The riding instructor at your school has given you a good grounding. Now, I want you to hold the neck strap along with your reins. That'll help you to keep your balance and save you from jabbing Pixie's mouth.'

We all watched as the Exmoor popped neatly over the first low pole and cantered on to the next. So absorbed were we that we did not notice the Colonel come up behind us until he spoke.

'So you've started my granddaughter jumping, eh?' He patted Jenny's uninjured shoulder approvingly. 'I'm glad to see you're training her in the right way. Make her cross her stirrups in front of the saddle next time round. Then she'll have to grip with her knees.'

While Pete and I watched with Jenny and the Colonel, we left Cavalier and Cloud tied to the fence. Suddenly we were amazed to hear the thud of hooves. We turned to see Benny cantering Cloud determinedly at the first of the jumps that Pete and I had been using.

'Benny!' Jenny shouted. 'Come back!'

'Give him a chance, Jenny,' said the Colonel as Benny thundered to the low brushwood. 'This should be interesting . . . See that!' he exclaimed as, with easy balance the gypsy boy cleared the jump. 'Blood will out. I don't suppose Benny's ever jumped a pony before in his life, but his instincts are taking over. He's his father's son, by Jove!' The Colonel was becoming quite excited as Benny put Cloud at the second fence. 'He's Rutland Reuben all over again. His father might have been a rogue, but he couldn't go wrong when it came to handling a horse.'

'All the same Benny ought not to have taken Cloud without permission,' Jenny said as he rode towards us.

'You're not the only ones that can jump, you see!' Sliding to the ground in front of us, Benny grinned at us cheekily as he made much of the mare.

'You'd no business to take Cloud without asking,' said Jenny. 'Anyhow, how long have you been here? Grandpa said you must report to us whenever you arrived at the stables.'

She would have said more but the Colonel surprisingly took Benny's part. 'Be fair, Jenny. This youngster has the makings of a horseman. If you're short of good material for the later summer shows you could do worse than enter him.'

Good for Benny, I thought. He wasn't easily daunted.

The rest of the afternoon was busy. Sergeant Sam had taken a group of seven riding on the heath. They returned at five o'clock and then we had to unsaddle the ponies, wipe over the tack and put it away. After that there was the usual routine of watering, feeding and hay-net filling.

'Be an angel and see to Sultan for me, Pippa.' Jenny called from the barn where she was supervising the doling out of the hay. 'Find Ernie and ask him to measure his feed.'

In the food store the stable-hand was giving out bran, chaff, and pony-nuts for Pete and Ian to feed to the horses. The boys left to take the feeds. I felt uneasy as I held out Sultan's bucket. Since receiving that horrible anonymous letter I was very much on my guard where Ernie was concerned.

'For Sultan, eh? We'll give him a few oats.' Ernie dug the scoop into the bin of oats and added bran and chopped hay. 'Now for some pony-nuts. Half a mo'. I'll just undo this fresh sack.'

He opened his penknife, slashed the stitching of the bag, put his knife away, ran the cubes over his fingers and measured out a quantity into the bucket.

Wonder of wonders, I thought, Ernie's making an effort to be pleasant! That was enough to arouse suspicion. Not wanting to linger, I picked up the bucket quickly and turned to go.

'Hold on a minute.' Ernie grasped the bucket handle and dived his other hand into the feed. 'Best give it a bit of a stir round. There! We don't want Sultan getting colic, do we?'

I shivered. Not liking to be alone with the smirking Ernie, I hurried to the Arab's loose-box. 'Good boy then.' I placed my free hand on Sultan's quarters. 'I expect you're ready for your supper.'

I tipped the mixture into the manger. Sultan blew gently at me and then dipped in his muzzle to eat.

Watching him, I lingered, patting his neck and talking to him to put off the moment when I would have to return the bucket to Ernie.

Sultan wuffled into the oats and bran, searching for his favourite pony nuts. Suddenly he snorted and threw up his head.

To my horror I saw scarlet staining the food in the manger.

'Oh no!' I gasped as I saw a jagged piece of glass glinting among the feed. Had the Arab bitten on the glass? I struggled to reach his head. Blood was dripping from his mouth.

'Help!' I called urgently. 'Somebody come quickly! Sultan's eating glass!'

Two pairs of feet raced over the cobbles. Ian appeared at the loose-box door but, quick though he was, Benny slipped past him and was first inside.

'Whoa! Steady there! Here, fellow. Let me see!' Grasping Sultan's mane the gypsy boy managed to pull down the Arab's head.

Ian moved to inspect the horse while I stood aghast at the blood which was still dripping from Sultan's mouth.

As Benny soothed the Arab and held his head still, Ian pulled back Sultan's lip, trying to see whether there was any glass still in his mouth.

I held my breath. 'Don't let him swallow,' I urged.

Ian succeeded in getting Sultan to open his mouth. 'It's all right. There's no glass there. There's plenty of blood but it doesn't look too serious—just a nick in the tongue. He'll be all right.'

Giving the Arab a reassuring pat he turned to me. 'How did it happen, Pippa?'

For an answer I removed the jagged glass from the Arab's feed. 'This was among his oats.'

Ian looked at it incredulously. 'How did it get there?'

Before my inner eye flashed the picture of Ernie running his hands through the feed to 'mix' it before letting me leave the food store. Had the stable-hand deliberately slipped the glass into the feed?

Was there no limit to his viciousness?

'Get Sergeant Sam right away,' I said to Ian. 'He ought to know what's going on!'

7

Ernie gets the sack

After checking that Sultan was in no danger, Sergeant Sam called all of the helpers into his tack-room office. Stern-faced, he looked from one to the other of us before asking: 'Just how did that piece of jagged glass find its way into Sultan's feed?'

'It must have been in one of the sacks from the corn merchant,' Ernie said glibly. 'Folks are shockingly careless these days.'

'Hmmm!' Sam Harrington's eyes half-closed as if he was considering that possibility. 'But supposing that was the case, how do you account for the fact that you didn't notice it? Surely you would have seen it in the scoop.'

Ernie jerked his head towards me. 'Better ask her,' he said treacherously. 'Nothing would suit her ladyship but that she should measure out Sultan's feed herself. Proper careless she is! Remember how she didn't fasten Sultan's loose-box, the day he got out and fell in the ditch. Then it was her job to clean the tack the evening before Jenny had her accident.

Reckon she hadn't checked the stirrup-leathers properly that day either.'

'Ernie! How could you!' I gasped. 'You know full well that it was you who measured out Sultan's oats. You put your hand into the bucket afterwards to make sure the feed was well mixed.'

'I can vouch for that,' Ian said quickly. 'I saw Ernie with his hands in the bucket as I came across the yard. I remember thinking at the time that it was an odd thing for him to do.'

'There was nothing odd about it.' Ernie stared challengingly at him. 'Sultan bolts his food, so with him being so important to the stables, I didn't want to risk him getting colic.'

'Nonsense!' said Jenny. 'Sultan's never bolted his food in his life.' She turned to Sergeant Sam. 'That's so, isn't it, Grandpa?'

'I've certainly never noticed any such tendency,' Sam Harrington confirmed. He looked hard at Ernie. 'I can't understand why you never felt the glass when you put your hand in the food.'

'I can tell you why.' I was unable to contain my anger any longer. 'The reason Ernie didn't discover the glass was because he put it there. That's what he must have been doing when he put his hand in the bucket and pretended to mix the feed.'

'Making wild accusations is slander, that's what it is,' Ernie bluffed.

'I'm not satisfied, Topsall,' Sergeant Sam said firmly. 'I've been watching you for some time. You've glibly laid the blame on other people too often. So you can get your coat and go. I'll send you a cheque for your money in the post.'

'Wrongful dismissal!' Ernie countered. 'That's what it is. I'll have you up before the tribunal, Sergeant Harrington. It'll cost you a thousand or two.'

Just then Emma came running from the house to see if there was any chance of another ride before bedtime. Rags was with her and, in her excitement at seeing us all together, Emma let his lead slip through her fingers.

The terrier pup saw Ernie, recognised him as a tormentor and ran at him with a baby snarl.

'Set your blinking dog on me, would you?' Ernie caught the pup in the side with his shoe.

'Take that, you lout!' Ian landed a well-aimed blow on Ernie's jaw.

'Assault, as well!' Ernie grunted. 'I'll have the law on the lot of you.'

'And we'll have the RSPCA on you,' Pete exclaimed over his shoulder, as he bent to examine the pup with Emma. Rags had escaped any real injury.

'You're a bad type, Topsall,' said Sergeant Sam. He drew himself up and added: 'I dare say the police might be interested in what you did to Sultan. Malicious wounding of an animal is against the law.' He jerked a thumb to the door. 'Get out!'

I felt like cheering!

But I didn't feel so triumphant when Pete and I were setting off for home the following evening and

I saw Ernie astride his motor-bike at the end of the lane.

Was he waiting for us?

'Try not to take any notice of him.' Pete's voice was hoarse with apprehension. 'If he says anything, ignore it!'

However, we had gone only a few metres when we heard the sound of Ernie's motor-bike starting up. He roared past us, did a U-turn and then slowed down behind us, 'walking' his feet along the ground while the motor-bike engine ticked over. He kept steadily beside us as we walked towards home.

'I can't stand this,' I whispered to Pete. 'What do you think he's going to do?' I looked towards the games field of the Comprehensive School. 'Shall we take a short cut through there?'

'And have Ernie chase us across open ground?' said my twin. 'Not on your life. We're safer sticking to the main road. There are too many people about for him to try anything on.'

Next morning, when Pete and I left home to go to Stableways, Ernie was waiting a short way up the road. As soon as we emerged from the front gate he zoomed level. He kept pace with us in the same nerve-racking way until we reached Stableways.

So it went on all that week. We didn't say anything to our parents or Sergeant Sam in case they might think it dangerous for us to continue going to Stableways, but we were scared. By Saturday, though, it seemed that Ernie had tired of his threatening behaviour. There was no sign of him when we left home in the morning. No sign, either, of him and his motor-bike on the main road. When we reached Stableways, Pete heaved a sigh of relief.

'There you are, Pippa. Ernie realises he can't scare us, and so he's given up. Let's hope he'll find something better to do with his time.'

Sergeant Sam was waiting by the tack-room door.

'I've just had a phone call to say that there'll be three extra for this morning's ride. I'd like you two to go across to the far field and bring up Briony, Galahad and Cinders.'

Emma, who had been hopefully hanging round the stable in jodhpurs, jersey and crash cap, must have overheard.

'Let me go too,' she pleaded. 'If there are three ponies, I can catch one.'

'Fair enough,' agreed Sergeant Sam. 'Cinders is only a small pony, so you can lead her, Emma. Better take bridles. You'll have to bring the ponies under the by-pass.'

With a handful of pony-nuts in our pockets, catching the three ponies was no problem; nor was slipping their bridles over their head collars.

Pete took the bay pony, Galahad. I took blue roan Briony and Emma led Cinders as Sergeant Sam had suggested.

Just over ten hands high, Cinders was a darling. She was rotund from the spring grass and mealy-nosed with a white star on her brown face. She had a rumpled black mane and Emma loved her on sight.

'Please give me a leg up,' Emma begged when I had inspected the fitting of Cinders' bridle to make sure she had not buckled the throat-lash too tightly. 'I want to ride her to the stables.'

'You can't do that,' I said firmly. 'Sergeant Sam said we were to lead the ponies.'

'That's right,' said Pete. 'Nobody sensible ever rides near the by-pass without a saddle.'

'Pooh!' Emma scoffed. 'It's safe enough. We go under the subway, don't we?'

'Yes, but we have to go a little way along the cycle track to reach the subway,' Pete reminded her. 'That's why we have to be careful.'

For answer, Emma sprang on to Cinders' back, dug her heels into the pony's plump sides and set off across the field at a canter.

Briony and Galahad were bigger, all of fourteen hands. Moreover they were fresh and would not stand still. It took Pete and me valuable minutes to stop them circling. By the time we had managed— by undignified scrambling—to gain their backs, Emma had reached the far side of the field.

'Wait for us!' Pete yelled as Emma leaned from Cinders' back to pull open the gate on to the by-pass.

Emma waved gaily. 'See you at the stables,' she called. 'I'll leave the gate open for you.'

'Don't go on the road!' I shouted. But Emma was in no mood to hear. As Pete and I galloped after her, she turned Cinders on to the grass that divided the busy by-pass from the cycle track and began to canter towards the subway, two hundred and fifty metres ahead.

She might have made it without mishap if it hadn't been for Ernie!

Although Pete and I hadn't seen the dismissed stable-hand that morning, he must have been hanging around Stableways waiting to cause trouble. Now, being Saturday, he had a couple of his leather-jacketed friends with him. They revved their engines and rode their motor-bikes along the cycle track behind Emma.

Drawing alongside, they blared their horns. Cinders, with the whizzing by-pass traffic on the one side and the noisy motor-bikes on the other, was terrified out of her pony wits.

To make matters worse, Ernie swerved his machine on to the grass, riding as near to the pony as he possibly could without actually touching her.

Cinders gave a snort of fright, shied and, with Emma clinging round her neck, bolted towards the traffic on the by-pass.

8

Ian to the rescue

'After her!' Pete put Galahad into a gallop.

Clods of turf were flung back by the bay's heels, and mud spattered my face as I pounded after them.

Small though she was, Cinders was fast. Cat-like ears flattened, tail streaming, with Emma in the saddle, she galloped into the traffic before either Pete or I had a chance to reach her.

A car swerved. A lorry pulled up with a hiss of air-brakes. Tyres screamed on tarmac as drivers saw the terrified pony and child ahead of them.

Ernie, viciously excited by the success of his action, blew another blast on the horn of his motor-bike and, with a whoop, revved over the grass and into the traffic lane behind Emma and the bolting pony.

I dreaded what might happen. Cinders could cross the central reservation into the oncoming traffic. Then, ahead of her, a blue estate car pulled up sharply. Its doors opened and out leapt a man and a boy. They raced towards the bolting pony.

'Ian and his father! Thank goodness!' Pete gasped. He reined up Galahad and jumped to the ground.

As I halted Briony beside him, I saw the vet grasp Cinders' bridle. The pony slewed and tried to pull away, but Ian also was ready for her. He grabbed the other side of her bridle.

Looking scared, Emma unlocked her fingers from where she had them gripped in the pony's mane and slipped to the ground. I put a hand out to steady her as she sagged.

'My legs feel all wobbly,' Emma moaned and burst into tears.

*   *   *   *

When the first shock was over, two things stayed in my mind. One was the cruel twist of Ernie's mouth under his helmet and goggles as he turned to watch what might happen when Cinders bolted towards the oncoming traffic. The other was the yellow and black chequered helmet of one of his companions. I remembered that I had seen that helmet before, and the black leather jerkin with the figure '7' in a white circle on the back. I knew who had worn them—Colin Blackmoor!

I voiced my thoughts to Pete and Ian as we led the ponies under the subway and into the fields on the other side of the by-pass.

Pete nodded. 'Yes, I've seen Colin in that black leather jerkin. He used to wear it when he was riding

Ernie's bike on the old airfield. Come to think of it, he had a yellow-and-black helmet, too.'

I faced my twin across Briony's withers. 'Didn't you say Colin was getting a new motor-bike—a Suzuki?'

'Yes, he had it for his birthday last week,' Pete confirmed. 'He was showing it off to some of the other fifth formers after the athletics meeting.'

Ian nodded. 'I was too busy helping my Dad stop Cinders to get more than a glimpse of those idiots.' He bent to pick up Cinders' reins which Emma had let trail. 'But now I come to think of it, I did notice that the fellow in the yellow-and-black helmet was riding a brand-new bike.'

'It was a Suzuki,' I said positively. 'When they first came past us on the cycle track, before they revved up after Emma, I remember thinking what an expensive-looking machine it was and wondering how it came about that Ernie and his pals had so much money to spend.'

'I suppose Ernie got his bike on the never-never,' Pete grunted, 'and as for Colin—if it *was* Colin—his father's incredibly rich. His pocket is bottomless.'

'What are we saying?' Ian looked aghast from Pete to me. 'None of us like Colin, but would he really do anything as rotten as making Cinders bolt with Emma into the thick of the traffic?' They could have been killed.'

'It was Ernie who was the real villain,' I recalled. 'Colin—if it *was* Colin—and the other lout—the boy in the red helmet—hung back.'

'Well, we shall soon know, or at least get a better idea,' Pete pointed out. 'Colin's due at the stables this afternoon. Sergeant Sam wants to see him go round the cross-country course again.'

'Yes,' agreed Ian 'and Colin's sure to turn up on his new bike. Then we can all have a hard look at his gear and find out if he definitely was one of the motor-bike gang.'

*   *   *   *

When Colin rode his motor-bike into the yard at Stableways that afternoon he was wearing a black-and-yellow helmet. But there was no black jacket with the number '7'. A blue leather bomber jacket, with a fur collar, topped pale stretch breeches and black rubber riding-boots.

'Look at his machine,' Pete whispered. 'It is a Suzuki, sure enough.'

'With an L-plate,' Ian pointed out. 'There was no L-plate on the machine this morning.'

'Just the same I'm sure it was Colin.' I said, looking at the sleek-haired boy with dislike.

Just then Sergeant Sam brought Sultan out of his loose-box. 'Here you are,' he called to Colin. 'Let's have you up on top. I'm giving you one more chance to show what you can do over the cross-country course.'

'Hear that?' Pete turned to Ian. 'It sounds as if Sergeant Sam's a bit disillusioned with Colin's

60

jumping. You might well be the one to ride Sultan at Boxheath, after all.'

Pete, Ian and I stood in a group with Benny and Jenny. Emma wasn't there, which was only to be expected after her terrifying experience that morning.

Colin looked tense as he rode Sultan to the start of the cross-country course. The Arab was jogging nervously and flinching at familiar objects in a way that was quite unlike his usual self.

'Do you think he's still suffering from the effects of the itching powder?' I asked.

'I'm sure he isn't," said Ian. 'I had him out only last night to go through the dressage test again and he was as calm as custard.'

'That's right,' nodded Jenny. 'I was watching. The only thing troubling Sultan is Colin. Colin's even more strung up than usual about jumping and it's communicating itself to Sultan.'

Sergeant Sam gave the signal to start. Then they were off. Colin took the first jump too fast but Sultan sailed over with half a metre to spare. Now they were cantering up to the second fence which Sergeant Sam had made into a double-oxer. It was a high, wide jump and Colin couldn't afford to upset Sultan's timing. We ran down the field to see how they would fare.

Colin seemed to check Sultan a little way from the jump and to shorten his reins. Then, clapping his heels to the Arab's sides, he drove him forward. They were over and riding for the triple bar. Sultan was going at a hard gallop and we were only just in time to see him clear.

The course now followed the outskirts of the wood and there was a tricky double, in and out of the green lane. The going was slippery and Sultan seemed to hesitate as if to recover himself after the first obstacle. Colin hit him and the Arab, taken by surprise, jumped the second post and rails from a standing start—very high and wide.

Panting after them, we saw that Sergeant Sam had added to the difficulty of the next jump by widening the ditch on take-off. He had also placed sleepers on the landing side. Sultan took off in good time, spread himself and landed safely.

They were doing well but the increased difficulty of the course had rattled Colin. He jerked Sultan's head to turn too sharply. The Arab skidded, lost his balance and almost fell.

Scrambling to regain his foot-hold, Sultan's nostrils flared. There was foam on the butt of his bit and his coat was streaked with sweat. As we watched, Colin hit him again with his switch.

At my side Jenny bit her lip. 'Poor Sultan!' She was angry on her horse's behalf, 'That slip was Colin's own fault. He nearly brought Sultan down. Fancy taking it out on the horse!'

'It shows what a rotter he is,' Pete said as we scrambled over the fence and raced across the next field, taking a short cut to see what would happen at the bank.

Colin was now riding rigidly. His arms like

pokers, ham-fisted, he set the Arab at the most formidable obstacle of the course. Although he automatically increased his pace as he neared the bank, we could see that his heart wasn't in it. He drove Sultan on in a spiritless way, almost as if he was hoping the Arab would refuse.

Sultan came to within take-off distance and stopped, his feet slipping on the sticky, spring-wet ground.

Colin raised his switch again and cracked it down on the Arab's flanks. Sultan, thinking the cut was intended as a punishment, took off in a standing leap that must surely have jarred the base of Colin's spine. The Arab's fore-feet gained the bank and, somehow, he managed to bring his hind-feet up to join them. Then, obviously not wanting to risk further punishment, he hurled himself over the post-and-rails, jumping in a wide arc to clear the bank and its drop at the same time. Colin then became totally unbalanced. He rolled off Sultan's back and fell to the ground. Still holding the Arab's reins he brought the horse down with him.

By twisting his body as he fell, Sultan managed to avoid landing on top of Colin, but, as the horse scrambled to his feet, his near-hind struck Colin on the forehead.

'Gosh!' gasped Ian. 'That was a nasty one.'

Shocked, Jenny, Ian, Pete and I hurried to Colin's side while Benny ran to catch Sultan who was standing trembling, reins trailing, a little way off.

'Colin is out cold,' Ian declared, taking off his

63

jacket to lay over the injured youth. 'He mustn't be moved.' He straightened to call to Sergeant Sam who was hurrying down the field. 'I'm afraid it's bad, sir. Better phone the doctor.'

9

An unwelcome inspection

'We'll have to X-ray Colin to check that there's no fracture of the skull,' the doctor explained. 'I'll get him to hospital right away.'

Pete pulled open the gate for the ambulance men to carry through the stretcher. Meanwhile Colonel Lyall hurried indoors to telephone the news of the accident to Colin's father.

Just then an estate car drove into the yard. I recognised the man at the wheel as Major Rotherham, a local horsy celebrity. He had once jumped for Britain and was now Pony Club Commissioner, Chairman of the Riding Club and a leading member of the Boxheath Trials Committee.

Stepping out of his car he took in the scene at a glance, then looked from the doctor to Sergeant Sam. 'It seems I've arrived at a moment of crisis. Is there any way I can help, or is everything under control?'

'All taken care of, sir,' Sergeant Sam said. 'I'll direct the ambulance out of the yard and then I'll be with you.'

The doctor drove away behind the ambulance and the rest of us waited in an awkward group a little distance from Major Rotherham who, to our bewilderment, produced a pocket-pad and ball-point and began to jot down notes.

'Ah, there you are, Mr Harrington.' The Major looked up as Sergeant Sam came back. 'I don't like to add to your troubles, but I have to explain that I'm here officially on behalf of the local authority.'

'Indeed, sir?' Sergeant Sam prompted stiffly.

'Yes, Mr Harrington. A complaint has been received about the alleged lack of safety standards at these riding stables. I've been asked to make an inspection.'

The news must have been as shattering to Sam Harrington as it was to the rest of us, and his face became wooden.

'Very well, sir,' he said at last. 'Firstly, I expect you'll want to know how the accident happened.' He explained briefly how Colin had lost his balance and fallen.

'It wasn't Sultan's fault.' Jenny was quick to defend her horse. 'It was the way he was ridden.'

The Major's face was blank. 'I think I ought to have a look at the animal.'

We all watched tensely as he spoke to Sultan, examined his mouth and then ran his hands down each leg in turn before picking up his feet. Next he inspected the Arab's bridle.

He turned to Sergeant Sam. 'Would you please remove the saddle?'

While Benny held Sultan's head, Sergeant Sam thrust his head under the nearside saddle-flap and unbuckled the girth. Folding the webbing over the seat he held the saddle for the Major to see.

'May I ask, sir, whether the complaint that you received was in connection with the equipment?' Sergeant Sam asked.

The Major looked up from his scrutiny of the girth and stirrup-leathers. He tested the near-side safety-bar before replying: 'The complaint was not specific. It was more in the manner of a general allegation. As I said, it concerned the lack of safety standards. It also mentioned the lack of experience of your helpers.'

So it seemed we were to blame, I thought!

How unfair when we had all done our best—and how rotten for Sergeant Sam and Jenny, who had always supervised our jobs around the stables! I wanted to put the blame where it really belonged— with Ernie Topsall. But I realised that if I spoke up now, I might only make things worse.

Sergeant Sam must have been thinking on the same lines because, just then, he gave us all a severe look as though warning us to keep quiet.

'I recently had to sack my stableman,' he told the Major, 'but even though we're short-handed, I do assure you that all rides are accompanied and everything is properly supervised.'

Ian, as the eldest, decided he could help at this point.

'Sergeant Sam is a stickler for safety, sir.'

'Yet there have been at least two quite serious accidents in the last fortnight.' The Major let his gaze rest deliberately on Jenny's sling. 'How do you account for that?'

'Jenny fell because somebody cut through one of the stirrup-leathers,' Pete told him.

The Major's eyebrows shot upwards.

'Did they now?' He looked thoughtfully at my twin. 'Are you sure it was a deliberate cut or could it have been wear and tear? Leather soon rots if it's not cleaned properly, you know.'

'My helpers check the tack every night,' Sergeant Sam told him. 'Everything is wiped over before being put away. Twice a week we have a general tack-clean and then I inspect it all.'

'In that case,' said the Major, 'you won't mind my going through every item for myself.'

Ian, Pete and I lifted the bridles from their pegs, and Major Rotherham went over them closely, testing straps and inspecting the bits. All seemed well until he came to Cloud's bridle which I had cleaned the previous evening.

I had checked it thoroughly before I hung it up, but now I noticed that the Major was scratching at the loop of the cheek-strap where it was attached to the bit. As I watched he lifted the end with his finger nail. To my horror the loop came away!

'The stitches are worn through.' He turned from me to Sam Harrington. 'This is the sort of thing that can lead to an accident. The bit would come out of the pony's mouth and the rider's control would be

68

gone . . . How often do you send your tack to the saddler?'

'That bridle was re-stitched three months ago.' Sergeant Sam peered to look. Then he turned reproachfully to me. 'You should have noticed this when you put the bridle away, Pippa. Why didn't you report it?'

'It wasn't like that then.' I turned desperately to the Major. 'Are you sure the stitching hasn't been snipped through with scissors?'

'We'll probably never know.' Major Rotherham looked thoughtful. 'Standards are slipping these days. General slackness! I suppose it's just possible that the saddler might have used old thread. That's something every horse-owner has to beware of.'

Without further comment he turned to the saddles where they stood on their racks. The Major looked keenly at each one, inspecting the stirrup-irons and the girths and turning them over to see whether the linings were clean.

I held my breath as he came to Cloud's saddle. I knew that the grey pony's bridle had been in good order when I put it away the previous evening. I was sure that the stitches had been deliberately unpicked. Whoever had done it must have known that an inspector would be coming. What could the culprit have done to the saddle? The Major turned it over. The inside was greasy and covered with hairs. It looked as if it hadn't been brushed for a month. Yet I had brushed it before putting it on the rack. I always did.

'I just don't believe it!' I said in dismay. 'That saddle was perfectly clean when I put it away last night.'

Everybody seemed to look at me in disbelief. I felt terrible. Why, there was doubt even in Pete's eyes!

10

Benny is banned

Colonel Lyall had returned from telephoning in time to witness my disgrace.

'I may not be at the stables all the time,' he told Major Rotherham, and Sergeant Sam, 'but I happened to be here with my young granddaughter yesterday evening. I saw Pippa clean that saddle and I particularly noticed how meticulously she brushed the lining.' He looked at the greasy serge surface. 'I can assure you that she did not leave it in that dirty condition.'

Pete moved forward to take a closer look. 'Let me see, sir.' He scraped a fingernail over the serge lining. He turned to Major Rotherham holding up his finger, the tip of which was now coated with a greasy, yellow substance. 'This could be vaseline, sir.'

'With a few hairs from the curry comb deliberately mixed in to make it look convincing.' Ian, in his turn, was now scrutinising the dirty lining.

Major Rotherham glanced from Pete and Ian to me, then to the Colonel and Sergeant Sam, before teasing up the greasy surface with his own fingernail. 'Hmm! The boys could be right,' he said. 'I suppose we'll have to give this young lady the benefit of the doubt, Mr Harrington. It seems as though some very strange happenings are taking place in your stables.'

'That's true, sir,' conceded Sergeant Sam.

'We knew there was sabotage,' Jenny burst out, 'but we thought Ernie Topsall was behind it all and that it would stop when he was sacked.'

'But it didn't,' said Ian. 'This shows there's still someone malicious at work, someone who wants to ruin Stableways' reputation.'

'That's right.' I turned to the Major. 'Could it have anything to do with the person who made the complaint?'

'It would be helpful to know,' added Sergeant Sam as the Major hesitated.

'I'm not at liberty to disclose the name of the informant,' Major Rotherham said with formal correctness, 'but, off the record, I don't think it likely.'

'There's just one possibility then,' the Colonel reluctantly glanced towards Benny.

'Don't look at me!' Benny protested quickly. 'Just because I was had up once, doesn't mean I'd play dirty tricks on the stable now. Sergeant Sam's been good to me. I wouldn't let him down—nor my mates.'

'Hmph! grunted the Colonel. 'The fact of the matter is, Benny, that I was thinking about your

72

one black mark only this morning because my granddaughter, Emma, told me that a nearly-empty bag of puppy-meal was missing.'

'It wasn't me,' Benny flustered.

'I'd like to believe you,' the Colonel told him.

'Show the Colonel,' Sergeant Sam urged Benny. 'Turn out your pockets.'

'Why should I?' Benny shifted his feet, and now we all looked at him suspiciously.

'Come on, Benny,' prompted Ian. 'Come clean.'

In a shame-faced way, Benny dived into the deep pockets of his over-large jacket and brought out two handfuls of broken puppy-meal, which he placed on the bench.

'It was for Tip, my lurcher.' He sounded forlorn. 'My step-dad doesn't give me any money to feed her.'

'Taking what doesn't belong to you is always wrong,' the Colonel reproved. 'If you'd asked Emma I dare say she'd have given you some biscuit for the bitch. In the circumstances—' he turned to Sergeant Sam '—I don't see that you've any option but to ban the boy from the stables. The least this proves is that he's untrustworthy.'

Sergeant Sam looked hard at Benny and I could see the struggle going on behind the old soldier's leathery face. He was sorry for Benny, I knew, but at the same time, he couldn't condone the petty theft.

'You're not to come here for the next week, Benny.' Sam Harrington pronounced sentence.

'That'll give us time to see if the trouble stops.' He turned to Major Rotherham. 'Are you satisfied with your inspection, sir?'

'Not entirely,' the Major said. 'I was asked to look into a complaint about the safety standards in this establishment. I arrive to find a serious accident. Now I hear about a pattern of malicious wrong-doing that could easily cause further accidents.' He glanced at Jenny's sling. 'By your own telling, one such quite serious mishap was brought about in precisely that way. I can only report to the authorities what I've found to be the case.'

'Stay your hand, James.' The Colonel spoke to Major Rotherham as a close friend. 'I'll vouch for Mr Harrington's integrity. I've known him for thirty-eight years and I can tell you that his standards have always been of the highest.'

'Yes, but we're none of us getting any younger,' the Major pointed out. 'Mr Harrington's eye might not be as keen as it used to be.'

Sam Harrington drew himself up, and said stiffly: 'There's nothing wrong with my eyesight, sir; nor with my judgment.'

'Come off your high-horse, Sam,' said the Colonel. 'The Major here will do his best to help you. Won't you, James?' Before Major Rotherham could reply the Colonel went on: 'I, too, may be old, but I'm no fool, either. Between us, Mr Harrington and I will get this thing straightened out. So if I give you my word that I'll be personally responsible for oversee-ing the running of the stable, will that do? If I'm wrong, I'll do what I've been putting off for the last six months—sell the place for building land, see that the horses go to suitable owners; find young Jenny a place in another riding establishment and put Sergeant Sam out to grass.'

'I'll do my best to give you time.' Major Rotherham's tone was still stern as he looked round at us. 'Get this straight, all of you. From this moment on, nothing else—repeat *nothing*—must be allowed to go wrong at Stableways. Is that clear?'

*   *   *   *

I didn't sleep well that night. I was too worried about the threat to Stableways. I heard the clock in the hall strike several times. I kept drifting into an uneasy doze only to become fully awake again with the Major's words going through my brain. Nothing, but nothing, else must be allowed to go wrong.

Suddenly I realised that something could be going badly wrong at that very moment!

In the upset of Major Rotherham's inspection I couldn't remember putting the padlock on the gate into the home field. The old padlock was rusty. Sergeant Sam had bought a replacement and asked me to be sure to put it on the gate before I went home. Since all the vandalism in the district and the outbreak of sabotage at Stableways, Jenny's grandfather had made a point of keeping all gates securely locked. At this very moment one of them could be hanging partly open and if the ponies pushed their way through and strayed, it would be my fault.

I must check. I quickly put on jeans and a sweater and sped through the sleeping avenues to Stableways.

The padlock wasn't on the tack-room window-ledge where I thought I'd left it, so I ran to the gate of the home field. The padlock was in place.

Thank goodness! I must have secured it after all.

Then I noticed that the gate on the far side of the field—the one leading into the jumping paddock—was open and the ponies had gone!

Running forward, I saw that the jumps had been smashed; poles, brushwood and the wooden bricks from the wall lay scattered across the ground. The vandals had struck again!

A jet was roaring across the sky as I stared at the chaos. As the noise faded I heard a pony squeal from near the spinney, followed by the angry barking of a dog. Then came the sound that I had learned to dread so much—the revving of a motor-bike engine. So those responsible were still here! I clambered on to the hedge bank to see.

Ponies were stampeding in the field beyond the spinney. An Alsatian was snapping at their heels and, as the ponies turned to escape the dog, two motor-bikes were churning ruts into the ground as they wheeled in a mad rodeo round-up.

Torn between a rash impulse to race over the fields to protect the ponies and the more common-sense need to summon help, I lingered, horrified.

Then a movement at my back made me turn my head sharply. I jumped down from the bank to see Pete.

'You took some tracking down,' he grumbled breathlessly. 'I got up early to go for a jog, looked out of the window and saw you disappearing round the corner of Laburnum Avenue. What's going on?'

'See for yourself,' I gasped. 'Two idiots are frightening the ponies in the far field.'

'Run back to the cottage,' said Pete. 'Alert Sergeant Sam, tell him what's happening and dial 999.'

11

Dial 999

It did not take Sergeant Sam long to pull a pair of old army trousers over his pyjamas and to struggle into a sweater. Then he and I hurried to help Pete rescue the ponies while Jenny dialled 999 and waited for the police to arrive.

Meanwhile, as Sergeant Sam and I neared the spinney we saw the ponies still galloping round the field, frightened. Two were making for the open gateway to the road and Pete was sprinting to head them off. He managed to turn one but the other clattered on to the roadway before my brother could reach the gate.

'Don't run after Turpin,' Sergeant Sam shouted urgently to Pete. 'If he thinks he's being chased, he'll only gallop off. If we leave him to himself the chances are he'll pull up and start to graze the verge.'

Meanwhile the other four ponies had stopped cantering around the field. One by one they dropped their heads to crop.

Sergeant Sam went round each of the remaining

sweat-streaked ponies as they grazed. 'Bracken, Daydream, Nibbles.' He spoke their names to calm them as he looked for injury. 'Soldier.' He came to the last of the four, a dark chestnut with white socks who was one of the entrants for the Boxheath Trials. 'What's this?' He ran a questing hand down the pony's near-fore. 'I don't like the look of this fetlock. It's puffy.'

'Is it bad, Mr Harrington?' Pete asked. We awaited the verdict in suspense—with just over a week to go to the Trials an injury to one of the competitors would be disastrous.

Sergeant Sam sighed as he straightened up from his inspection. 'The fetlock's badly swollen and there's heat in the joint. It could have been caused by a kick or a stone. Soldier will be out of the Trials, that's for sure!'

'Oh dear!' As I spoke, I realised that one of the other ponies, a grey, was now standing awkwardly, resting his off-hind. Sergeant Sam also noticed and, leaving Soldier for the moment, returned to the grey.

'Nibbles. Here fellow ... Now, how did I miss that?' He fingered the rapidly-swelling lump on the point of the pony's hock. 'It seems as if this was caused by a blow from a stone.' Sergeant Sam straightened. 'Now to catch Turpin.'

As we'd expected, the black pony had pulled up as soon as he realised he was no longer being followed. He was standing in the gateway of the local cricket ground. His head was down. Flecked with drying sweat, he was shivering. He looked utterly dejected. He did not even raise his head when Sergeant Sam spoke to him.

'What is it, fellow?' Sergeant Sam was about to pat Turpin's neck but he stopped with an angry gasp at the sight of blood oozing from a gash on the pony's withers. 'Those vandals ought to be thrashed.' Hands shaking with rage, he threaded a leading rope through the D of Turpin's head-collar. Then he made a pad of his handkerchief and applied it to the gash. Pete and I added our handkerchiefs but still the blood soaked through.

'Those hooligans must have hit him with a broken bottle.' Sergeant Sam's face set grimly as he led the pony back into the field. 'I'll take him straight back to the stables and call the vet. You two follow with Nibbles and Soldier. All three ponies will have to be kept up, of course.'

We felt dreadful as we led the injured animals towards Stableways. Soldier, Nibbles and Turpin were to have taken part in the under-sixteen cross-country and dressage events at Boxheath. John Gregg, Billy Lane and Amanda Howe, who should have ridden them, were all more experienced than Pete and I. They would have much better chances of doing well in the Trials. Now only Cloud, Cavalier and Sultan were left to represent Stableways. Ian might do well with Sultan, I thought, but it was doubtful whether Pete and I were good enough to win rosettes.

Desperately I turned to Pete. 'What now? Do you

think we ought to drop out of the Pairs and let two of the others ride Cloud and Cavalier? They're much better riders than we are.'

'That wouldn't help,' said Pete. 'They're over the age limit for the Junior Pairs.'

'I'd forgotten that.' I felt suddenly appalled that so much depended on Pete and me. 'It'll be up to Ian and us to try to bring success to Stableways.'

'I know.' Pete looked shattered. 'Daunting, isn't it?'

By now we were within sight of the stable-yard and we could see Jenny talking to two policemen who were getting out of a panda car. As we led the ponies through the gateway one of the policemen came up to Sergeant Sam.

'Sorry about the delay, sir. We were held up by a road traffic accident, and we're short-handed because there's a demo later this morning.'

'So you've hardly got time to follow up a complaint about injuries to ponies, I expect,' Sergeant Sam said reasonably. 'Especially as you'll be busy with the Prime Minister's visit tomorrow.'

'Even so, we'll do our best,' said the constable. 'Now, what precisely is the complaint?'

'See for yourself.' Sergeant Sam's tone was grim as he raised the handkerchief pad from Turpin's wound. 'Some vandals have used a knife or a broken bottle on this animal.'

'And they lamed these two with stones,' Pete put in from between Soldier and Nibbles.

81

'Where are these villains now?' asked the policeman.

'Back in their homes, I expect, with their bikes in their garages,' Sergeant Sam grunted as he again staunched Turpin's gash. 'If you hurry you might find that their motor-bike engines are still warm and their boots covered in mud from the field.'

'So you can definitely identify them?' queried the constable. 'You saw them clearly enough to recognise them?'

'Well, no,' Sam conceded. 'By the time we reached the field, they were just two black shapes with an Alsatian dog streaking behind them.'

'Even though you couldn't identify them, sir, have you grounds for suspecting someone?' the policeman prompted.

'Yes, I have,' Sergeant Sam said firmly. 'A youth by the name of Ernie Topsall, my former stableman, and one of his mates.' Sergeant Sam recounted Ernie's other vicious exploits.

'Right,' the policeman said briskly. 'We'll follow this up immediately.'

Later that morning, Ian's father, the vet, declared that none of the injured ponies would be fit to compete at Boxheath. He stitched Turpin's wound, injected him with anti-tetanus serum and a shot of antibiotic. Then he gave Soldier and Nibbles antitetanus jabs, too, and prescribed antiseptic cream for their injuries.

Meanwhile we were all in suspense. Had the police arrested Ernie? Jenny and Ian were fuming over the injuries to the ponies and so were John, Billy and Amanda, who were to have ridden in the Trials.

'The police can't have picked up Ernie and his mate,' Pete said at last, 'or we would have heard something by now. They'd have been sure to contact Sergeant Sam to get him to lay charges.'

'There's no point in brooding about it, Pete,' Jenny called as we worked with the others to repair the jumps. 'I want you and Pippa to give your mind to your practice.'

We rode badly, perhaps because we felt everyone was watching us critically, knowing that they could have done so much better.

Cloud and Cavalier sensed our nervousness. They became rattled and seemed to lose heart as the jumps clattered behind us. Finally Cavalier ran out at the hog's- back. Pete turned him and determinedly rode him back at the jump, but the pony had lost confidence. This time he stopped short and Pete flew over his head to land in the middle of the brushwood.

Gamely, my brother scrambled back into the saddle, knowing that his mount could not be allowed to get away with such behaviour. When a pony was allowed to refuse it was apt to become a habit.

I wheeled Cloud and rode her alongside Cavalier. Usually it was Pete who set the pace in our jumping. This time I knew it was up to me and the mare to give the lead.

'Come on, Pete,' I encouraged. 'Keep together.'

Side by side we put our mounts into a canter. They were so close that their shoulders were almost touching. I could sense Cavalier hesitate at the take-off. Impulsively I leaned across to grab his rein.

Pete laid his riding stick along the other side of the pony's neck. Hemmed between Cloud and the stick, Cavalier had no alternative but to jump.

'Well done,' called Jenny as we landed safely. 'Now turn the ponies and take the fence again.'

After that we did better. It seemed as though the challenge had taken our minds off the spectators. Now we were able to jump our best.

Then, as we reined up after a triumphant round we were agog to see another police car draw up in the stableyard.

'Now to hear that Ernie's been put behind bars!' I said.

'You hope.' Pete was sceptical. 'The police don't get results as quickly as that except on television.'

Dismounting, we pressed forward with the others to hear what the policeman had to tell Sergeant Sam. We were forestalled because, after a brisk word, Sergeant Sam led them into the cottage and firmly shut the door on us.

After about twenty minutes, they came out again and the policeman drove away leaving Sergeant Sam at the doorway.

'Anyone been arrested, Mr Harrington?' Ian asked eagerly.

Sergeant Sam looked impatient. 'I'm not sure the police want me to tell you about their investigations.'

'Oh, come on, Grandpa,' coaxed Jenny. 'We'll all swear not to say anything to anyone else.'

'Spill the beans, Mr Harrington,' urged Billy Lane. 'We've got a right to know.'

'Well, it isn't particularly good news, what there is of it so far,' said Sergeant Sam. 'Ernie Topsall's mother swears that he was still in bed when the vandalism took place.'

'What about his motor-bike?' prompted Pete. 'Wasn't the engine still warm—and wasn't there any field mud on Ernie's boots?'

'The policeman didn't say.' Sergeant Sam shrugged. 'But then there's no reason why they should tell me everything.'

'What about the Alsatian?' I asked.

'Ah, the dog did give them a bit of a lead,' said Sergeant Sam.' It seems that one of Ernie's motor-bike mates does have an Alsatian. They questioned the dog's owner—'

'Who was he?' interrupted Amanda.

'They didn't say, but like Ernie he's got an alibi. He said he was still in bed at the time and his mother and elder sister confirmed his story.'

'They're all lying,' said Pete.

'That's as maybe,' said Sergeant Sam. 'But, without proof, what can the police do? The constable said he'd given both of them a stern warning and he advised me to alert all my helpers to keep their eyes open—not to let any strangers on the premises— and either to stable all the ponies or keep them in the home-field.'

*　　*　　*　　*

For the next few days we were all on our toes. Sergeant Sam and the Colonel took it in turns to keep watch at night. Cloud and Cavalier were stabled where nobody could interfere with them and spoil their chances for Boxheath.

We all had to work hard. Without Benny and Colin, with no stableman and with Jenny's arm still in its sling, Sergeant Sam was very short of help. There was plenty for everyone to do. Even so, Pete and I managed to get in our jumping practice. We must have been improving because Jenny was quite pleased.

'Even if you don't win rosettes you should put up a creditable show,' she told us after a particularly successful session on Saturday evening.

The Boxheath event was now very near and Ian, too, was putting in a lot of practice. He rode Sultan several hours a day, keeping the Arab fit by roadwork, putting him round the cross-country course and carrying out dressage tests under Sergeant Sam's keen eye. The pair were doing well. Ian's dressage was acquiring polish.

The only snag was Emma's dog, Rags, who seemed to have taken a great liking to Sultan. Although Emma was supposed always to keep him on a lead when she was around the stables, he often slipped out of the house. Whenever the Colonel's housekeeper opened the back door, there was Rags.

He would dash between her ankles, and make his escape.

One morning Ian did not turn up at Stableways at his usual time. There was a phone call from him to say that his father's receptionist had 'flu and that he was needed to help with the animal patients. So it fell to Pete and me to see to Sultan.

I filled the Arab's hay-net to occupy him while I removed the soiled bedding-straw and Pete prepared his main feed. Leaving Sultan contentedly pulling at his hay I went out of the loose-box to fetch the stable-fork. I couldn't have shut the door behind me because, when I came back, I saw the tip of a white tail whisking round the edge of the loose-box door.

'Rags!' I called in alarm. 'Come out of there.'

I hurried forward, afraid that the Arab might take fright at having the small animal so near to his legs, and that Rags might be kicked.

To my surprise, no sound came from inside the loose-box. I had expected snorts and squeals from Sultan, followed by yelps of distress from Rags. But when I reached the door, an astonishing sight met my eyes. The little black-and-white puppy with the one brown ear and the brown patch over one eye was standing sniffing inquisitively at the Arab's foreleg while the horse, hay-net forsaken for the moment, turned his head, bent his neck and huffed gently at him.

I stood motionless. I was afraid to move in case I startled either of them. On the other hand I was still

87

scared that Rags, by a sudden movement, might upset the horse.

To my horror the terrier pup darted out a pink tongue to dab at the Arab's muzzle.

Sultan jerked up his head. For a heart-stopping moment he stood rolling a sideways eye at Rags. Then his ears swivelled forward. He dropped his head and returned the terrier's lick with a sweep of his own large tongue.

I tiptoed away, leaving them together while I fetched Jenny and Pete.

'Let Rags stay while Sultan has his feed.' Jenny was wise in the ways of horses. 'Then take him back to the house. Horses often make odd friendships but I don't think it would do for Rags to be at large in the stables when there are other animals about.'

'Too right,' sighed Pete. 'Cavalier, for one, can't stand dogs. Having Rags loose around the place could lead to a riot.'

Cloud and Cavalier jumped especially well that morning and Pete's and my spirits took to the air with the ponies. It was a lovely spring day. Daffodils were blooming in the grass around the Colonel's house and bright polyanthus blossomed in the window-boxes of Sergeant Sam's cottage. Primroses and violets nestled round the boles of the orchard trees and the young grass was springing green.

It wasn't until Emma came running from her grandfather's as we walked the ponies back to the stables that we had the first hint of anything amiss.

Emma's blonde hair had lost the bobble-clip that

held it in its pony-tail. Blowing wild, it added to the distress in her face. Her cheek had been scratched by a bramble. Her yellow anorak was grimy and her blue eyes brimming with tears.

'Rags is missing!' she sobbed.

'Perhaps he's gone to see Sultan,' I comforted hopefully.

Emma shook her head. 'No, I've looked. Oh dear, I do hope he hasn't strayed far.'

Pete jumped down from Cavalier. 'As soon as we've unsaddled the ponies we'll help you to search.'

To try to ease Emma's fears we pointed out that pups often got into scrapes. We reminded her that Rags had once been missing for a couple of hours, and then been found asleep in a basket of washing. Surely there was no need to be so upset.

How wrong we were!

12

Trapped!

By lunchtime Rags still hadn't been found.

Tearfully, Emma went into the house to lunch with her grandfather. Pete and I had planned a picnic in the tack-room. We were about to share out the pasties, apples and crisps which our mother had carefully packed when I caught sight of a folded sheet of paper, weighted by a stirrup-iron.

Pete peered over my shoulder to read:

'To whom it may concern. If Emma wants to see Rags again she must tell the Colonel to agree to Mr Blackmoor's offer to buy Stableways.'

For a moment Pete and I were too staggered to say anything.

'Who'd write such nonsense?' I puzzled at last.

'The same person who wrote the other anonymous note.' Pete said. 'Not Ernie, after all, but *Colin!* This time the idiot hasn't bothered to disguise his handwriting.'

'Yes, Colin came out of hospital a couple of days ago,' I said. 'That knock on the head must have affected his brain for him to write anything so dotty.

It's all so obvious. He's given himself away. Everybody knows his father would pay plenty to develop Stableways land. There are a hundred and twenty hectares. It's the only part of Dormhill that hasn't yet been built on. It would be worth a fortune to a greedy property developer.'

'Oh, gosh! A thought's just struck me.' Pete nearly choked on his Cornish pasty. 'I wonder if Colin is so crackers that he'd do Rags some harm.' He dashed into the yard. 'Come on. There may not be much time to lose.'

I followed him, leaving our lunch uneaten. 'What are we going to do?' I asked.

'Tackle the criminal lunatic!' Pete replied grimly.

*   *   *   *

Twenty minutes later, Pete and I panted up the drive of the Blackmoor's large Victorian house.

'What now?' I asked. 'Do we ring the front door bell?'

'No. First let's scout round for Rags,' Pete decided. He stared at the out-buildings beyond the bank of early flowering rhododendrons. 'Now where would Colin have hidden the pup? Perhaps in the old stables or the coach house.'

Keeping away from the house, we ran across the wallflower-edged lawn to the cover of some forsythia bushes. Then we made our way through the shrubbery to the back of the stable buildings.

'Sssh!' I gripped Pete's arm. 'I can hear whimpering.'

We held our breath to listen.

The sound came from one of the out-buildings!

Making sure no one was around, we crept along the side of the old stable-block to peer through the coach-house window. A shaft of dusty sunlight glinted on the winged radiator cap of a vintage Bentley. The car seem to take up most of the room. Beyond it the far corners were dark and it was difficult to see. However, I managed to glimpse a moving patch of white as the whimpering began again.

'Rags, it's all right. It's only us,' I whispered through the door.

Stealthily we inched open one of the double-doors. With a growl and a snarl, a white-and-brown dog that was a lot bigger than Rags came forward, menacing and ready to pounce.

In the half-light we could see that the dog was definitely not Rags!

It was a springer spaniel bitch. From the corner behind her came an urgent whimpering and squeaking. She had a box-full of young puppies who were protesting against the loss of their mother's warmth.

'Steady, old girl!'

Pete backed warily, but the bitch came on. Her snarls turned to a snapping of teeth and I edged towards the doorway.

At that moment the door banged shut. There

came the grating of a bolt on the outside followed by the click of a padlock.

'Got you this time!' mocked Colin Blackmoor's voice. 'Breaking and entering. That's what the police will call it.'

'You must be crackers to think you can get away with this.' Pete dodged the bitch's snapping jaws to shout through the door. 'That kick on the head must have driven you right round the bend.'

'No one but a complete idiot would have written that note,' I added. 'Who did you think you were fooling?'

'You pair for a start,' Colin scoffed. 'You walked right into the trap, didn't you?'

'Stop playing silly blighters, Colin.' Pete rattled the door. 'Let us out before your dog bites us.'

'You're only making things worse for yourself,' I added. 'Where's Rags?'

'Not here,' Colin said through the door. 'Since you're such clever sleuths, I'll let you work that one out for yourselves. So long! I'm leaving you in there until my father comes home. He's gone to the town to fix up about a burglar alarm. Someone broke in and stole the hub caps and radiator mascots from several of his vintage cars. Caught red-handed, aren't you?'

As Colin's footsteps died away the spaniel renewed her frenzy. Teeth bared, she advanced towards us even more menacingly.

'Quick, Pippa!' Pete half-lifted me on to the wing

of the vintage Bentley. 'Scramble on to the roof of the car.'

There was no time to think about the gleaming paint-work, nor about the sag in the old-fashioned fabric roof. We had to get out of reach of the spaniel's teeth.

Kneeling there, in the semi-dark, I noticed a chink of light overhead.

'Look, a trap-door!' I gasped.

The trap must have been unused for years. We pushed and shoved but it didn't move. Pete felt carefully all round the edges.

'There must be something holding it,' he groaned.

'Perhaps it's nailed up,' I said.

'You're right!' Pete's fingers encountered the shank of a rusty nail. 'Now, how are we going to get this out? Oh, I know! That multi-purpose pen-knife you gave me for Christmas, Pippa. The marlin spike should do it.' It seemed an age before Pete's prodding broke the rusty nail. 'Three more to go,' he reported as the village clock struck four.

But it was five o'clock before we scrambled into the hay loft above the Blackmoor's stables. We had just managed to run down the stairs into the tack-room, cross the yard and dodge behind the rhododendrons when Colin's father's Mercedes purred up the drive.

At the wheel we saw Mr Blackmoor. Sitting beside him was the Dormhill police inspector, in uniform and obviously on the job!

'What now?' I said, aghast to Pete. 'If we run

away we shall look guilty. What on earth are we going to do?"

13

What's happened to Sultan?

'Don't flap Pippa. The police Inspector may not be here because of us,' Pete pointed out. 'Perhaps Colin's father's brought him here to advise about the burglar alarms.'

'Yes, that's more likely,' I agreed. 'So let's find Rags. Emma won't sleep tonight if he's not back before her bedtime.'

'Right,' said Pete, 'Come on.' He forced a way through the shrubbery to the road. 'Colin is more cunning than we thought, so I don't think he'd bring Rags here after all.'

'Then where?' I puzzled.

'Perhaps he's taken the pup to Ernie's,' said Pete. 'We'll try there.'

When we reached the terraced house, we saw a motor-bike parked outside.

'Ernie's here,' Pete groaned. 'So it's no use trying the front door and asking Mrs Topsall about Rags.' He glanced towards an entry half-way down the street. 'Let's scout round the back.'

We made our way past dustbins to the rear of

Number 14. From the garage we could hear yapping. Rags was protesting at being imprisoned!

'It's a wonder he hasn't barked himself hoarse,' I said. 'What do we do now?'

Pete tried the gate, but it seemed that the latch was wedged.

'Let's not fall into another trap by trying to break in,' he said sensibly. 'Ernie's here with the dog. If we alert Sergeant Sam and the Colonel, they might be able to catch him red-handed. I'll stay on guard, while you find a phone box.'

There was a telephone kiosk at the end of the street. Hopeless! The windows had been smashed and the telephone cord dangled.

I asked a woman where the next phone box might be. She directed me to a post office four-and-a-half streets away, outside which, she said, there were two phone boxes. One of these had also been vandalised, but the other was working. I rang Sergeant Sam's number but the phone seemed to be out of order. So I had to ring the Colonel. It took me quite a while to convince him that Rags was being held captive in Ernie's house. It was almost half-an-hour later before I was on my way back to report to Pete.

As soon as I turned into the street I noticed that Ernie's motor-bike had gone from in front of the house, so I hurried through the entry to find my brother.

'I heard the bike rev up,' he confirmed. 'Ernie must have gone off for the evening, but Rags is still here and Mrs Topsall's in the house. She came into the yard a few minutes ago to peg out some washing.'

'In that case,' I said, 'I'll go to the front and keep watch ready for the Colonel and Sergeant Sam to arrive.'

I felt rather conspicuous loitering outside the Topsall's house and it seemed a long time before the Colonel's estate car drove down the street. As it pulled up I saw Emma sitting beside her grandfather. In the back was Sergeant Sam with, to my surprise, a police constable. It didn't take them long to explain to a flustered Mrs Topsall what had happened and for Emma to be rapturously reunited with Rags.

'Where is your son now, Mrs Topsall?' the constable asked.

'He said he was going for a "burn up", down the by-pass,' Mrs Topsall told him. 'That boy'll be the death of me, if he isn't the death of himself first. He's been nothing but trouble ever since his father went off with the barmaid from the Three Crowns. Ernie wasn't so bad when he had a job but since he got the sack he's gone from bad to worse. Out at the disco, off to the greyhounds, or round the pubs every night. Where he gets the money from, I don't know.'

The policeman brought out his pocket radio and spoke to the control room to ask them to warn all patrol cars to keep a look out for Ernie and his motor-bike.

*　　*　　*　　*

We thought Ernie was well and truly taken care of—but no! When we got to Stableways next morning to help with the final preparation for Boxheath the following day, we learnt from Jenny that both Ernie and Colin Blackmoor were missing. The Colonel and Sergeant Sam had been alerted to let the police know if they turned up at Stableways.

'I wonder why Ernie and Colin are both missing,' I puzzled. 'Have they gone off together, and why?'

'Well, we mustn't waste time chattering about that unholy pair,' Jenny said firmly as Ian came on the scene. 'Hi, Ian! It's all hands to the pump. More trouble! Vandals have made a gap in the hedge by the by-pass and Grandpa's having to make it up before any of the ponies stray into the traffic. Meantime there's Sultan to be clipped ready for the Trials tomorrow.'

'I can manage that,' Ian told her. 'Just stand by his head to keep him quiet.' He glanced at Jenny's sling. 'Think you can manage with the one hand?'

'I'll try. Sultan's usually as quiet as a fireside moggie. I don't think he minds being clipped.'

'Probably thinks it makes him look handsome,' said Pete.

'Meanwhile I'll clean the tack,' I volunteered.

'Super,' said Jenny. 'We want everything spotless and in good order for Boxheath. If Emma comes she can help you. One or two of the others said they'd be here later. We need all the help we can muster to put on a really super turn-out tomorrow.'

Pete and I started work in the tack-room. A few

minutes later we were startled to hear a cry of anguish from Sultan's loose-box. 'No!' Jenny was exclaiming in horrified tones. 'It can't be! It's just not true! Tell me I'm having a nightmare, Ian.'

Dropping saddle-soap and cleaning cloths on the tack-room bench, Pete and I ran to find out what was wrong. We saw Sultan standing in his loose-box. His rug was turned back and Jenny and Ian were gazing in appalled fascination at the crazy zig-zag pattern in which he had been clipped. Zebra stripes of bright-chestnut winter coat stood out against the darker background of his skin.

'Sabotage!' gasped Pete. 'Colin's and Ernie's last dirty trick before they went missing!'

'This explains where Ernie and Colin were last night,' I pointed out. 'Do you think we ought to ring the police and report?'

'I'll do it,' my twin volunteered. He glanced again at the Arab's disfiguring clip. 'From the way Sultan's been nicked with the clippers he'll take a bit of holding. Jenny can still use only one hand so she'll need your help.'

'Too true,' groaned Jenny. 'Poor Sultan's had such a scare that it's going to be quite a job to get anywhere near him with the clippers.'

Their worst forebodings were true. When Ian plugged in the electric clippers Sultan lashed out with his hind legs.

'Steady, boy.'

Jenny and I stood on either side of the Arab holding his head collar and soothing him while Ian approached cautiously. At the whirr of the clippers Sultan stamped restlessly and pulled against our hold. With the first touch of the metal on his side, Sultan went beserk. Twisting, snorting and kicking, he did everything he could to evade being clipped.

'It's no use, Ian,' Jenny said at last. 'We'll have to find Grandpa. Otherwise one of us will get hurt.'

Even when Sergeant Sam came into the loose-box to take over the clipping Sultan would not be soothed. It was impossible to put the clippers near him. Worse, each time the power was switched on the whirr of the electric motor seemed to drive him into a frenzy.

'Better leave it and try again this afternoon,' Sergeant Sam decided.

Just then a small shabby figure in an over-large jacket hesitantly approached across the court-yard—Benny!

'I was banned from here for a week, Mr Harrington.' The gypsy boy looked at Sergeant Sam pleadingly. 'The week's up, so I've come back to help.'

Sergeant Sam groaned and put his head in his hands. 'That's all I need!'

'Please don't be like that, Grandpa.' Jenny gazed hopefully at Benny. 'Give him a chance. None of us has been able to quieten Sultan. Let's see what a horse-whisperer can do.'

Benny looked at us eagerly. Then, ignoring Sergeant Sam's doubtful shake of the head, he moved forward to give Sultan's neck a soothing pat.

We held our breath as the Arab turned his head and huffed welcomingly at him. Benny blew back almost as if he were another horse greeting a stable-mate.

'Leave me alone with Sultan for a bit, mister,' Benny pleaded with Sergeant Sam. 'He won't harm me. Give me a chance.'

As we quietly filed out of the loose-box, we heard Benny softly crooning to the Arab. The horse-whisperer was back at work!

14

A fight in the horse-box

Miracle of miracles—Benny's magic worked!

'Steady boy. There's a good fellow. Over now. Whoa, there!'

The gypsy boy crooned as Sergeant Sam clipped.

There was one heart-stopping moment when Sergeant Sam came to a ticklish place under Sultan's tummy, but Benny gently lifted Sultan's near-fore so that the horse couldn't move without over-balancing. It was necessary only for him to hold up Sultan's fore-leg for a few moments. Afterwards the Arab stood quietly enough until the job was done.

Benny was well and truly back at Stableways, bringing us luck, it seemed, as he helped to thin manes, wash tails, and to groom the competing ponies until their coats shone.

Meanwhile, however hard I worked, I could not dismiss the unpleasant thoughts about Ernie and Colin. Where were they now? What were they doing? Planning more villainy or lying low?

'Oh, forget that pair, Pippa,' Pete said, reading my thoughts. 'Here you are riding for Stableways tomorrow at Boxheath. All your pony dreams are about to come true and you're letting your fury about Ernie and Colin make you unhappy.'

I forced the horrid pair from my thoughts but that did not stop me from having nightmares about them when I went to bed that night. So I was glad to be awakened early the following morning.

At Stableways we found Benny already at work, sewing the plaits into Cloud's and Cavalier's manes. He made himself useful in so many ways, blue-bagging Cloud's tail, replacing a slightly worn girth on Sultan's saddle, and being on hand to encourage the Arab and the others into the horse box.

At last we were on our way. Squashed in with Ian, Pete and Jenny beside Sergeant Sam, who was driving, I felt more nervous with every minute. True, the jumps in the Junior Pairs competition wouldn't be very big, but it would be a demanding course with tricky turns and obstacles. I desperately hoped we would be in good time so that we could walk round beforehand. Otherwise, I felt sure that I'd forget the order in which the jumps came and perhaps be disqualified.

The Colonel's estate car drew up beside us on the showground and Emma and her grandfather got out.

'Don't unbox the ponies yet,' the Colonel said to Sergeant Sam. 'They're better where they are until nearer the time to compete.' He glanced from Ian to Pete and me. 'Most important—you young people must report immediately to the secretary's tent to pay your entry fees and collect your numbers.'

'I'll stay with the ponies.' Benny made a dive for the back of the horse box, but Sergeant Sam was too quick for him.

'No, you don't.' He hauled the boy back. 'I want the animals to rest. You can come with us to the secretary's tent.'

There was a queue at the table, filling in forms and handing over the money and receiving change, so it must have been quite twenty minutes before we left the marquee and tied on our competitor's numbers. Then we made for the ring in which Pete and I were to compete. Sergeant Sam and the Colonel were drawing our attention to various points while Benny and Emma, wide-eyed with excitement, ran from jump to jump, pointing out possible pitfalls and giving us the benefit of their advice.

It was all well-meant, but I was beginning to get muddled.

'I don't think this is helping,' I whispered to Pete after Sergeant Sam had pointed out how many strides we would need to fit in between the two fences of the double. 'I wish they'd let us go round quietly by ourselves.'

'Chin up, Pippa,' Pete encouraged. 'Cavalier and I'll be beside you. If you're worried you can take your timing from us. The jumps aren't very different from the ones that we've been practising over.'

His words were lost in an unexpected and

alarming commotion. Somewhere a horse was squealing. Then the crowd of competitors and spectators were suddenly in an uproar!

We turned to see what was wrong.

'Lor', it's Sultan!' Benny exclaimed as Jenny's chestnut Arab bolted through the throng. Benny ducked under the rails and ran to try to catch the frightened horse. Ian and Sergeant Sam were close behind.

There were enough people chasing Sultan, so the rest of us hurried towards the horse box from which we could still hear squeals and whinnies followed by mysterious thumps.

When I reached the ramp just behind Pete I saw that two youths were scuffling inside—Colin and Ernie!

They were grappling around Cloud and Cavalier who, frightened, were pulling at their head-ropes. It was an incredible sight. How could anyone be so stupid as to fight round two ponies who were about to go into the show-ring? We just couldn't believe our eyes.

'Let me go, you fool!' Ernie was grunting as he struggled to throw off Colin's judo grip.

'Break it up, you lunatics!' Pete shouted, dashing up the ramp.

To my horror, I saw the glint of a knife in Ernie's hand.

'Look out!' I called to my brother.

As though Pete was scoring a goal, he kicked the knife from Ernie's grasp.

At that moment, Cavalier, terrified, lashed out with his hind-feet. His hooves caught Colin and Ernie and sent them hurtling out of the horse box. Colonel Lyall arrived on the scene as they landed at his feet.

The Colonel seized each of them by the hair and pulled them apart as two policemen came running up.

Sergeant Sam and Ian appeared through the astonished throng of bystanders. Sergeant Sam was leading Sultan and Benny was on the Arab's back, gentling his neck with both hands and whispering soothingly to the horse.

At that moment an announcement came over the tannoy.

'The Junior Pairs Jumping Class is about to begin. Competitor numbers three and four, eleven and twelve, and fifteen and sixteen into the collecting ring please.'

'That's us!' I gasped to my twin. 'Eleven and twelve. Come on!'

I hurried into the horse box to untie Cloud who shied away, still frightened.

'There, there!' I tried to use Benny's whispering technique. 'Calm down, girl.' As I patted the mare's neck, I noticed that her plaits were dangling. Anguished I turned to Jenny. 'What are we going to do? Ernie's cut out the thread and the ponies' manes are coming undone. There's no time to sew them again.'

As Pete led Cavalier down the ramp, Jenny called

Ian to help us. 'Pull the plaits right out. They're not all that important in a junior jumping class.'

'Sultan's mane will have to be plaited again for the dressage,' Emma pointed out.

'I can't sew with one wrist still in a sling,' Jenny said. 'But I remembered to bring a needle and thread in case any plaits came undone.' She handed her sewing case to Benny. 'Here, wonder-boy. You know how to cope!'

Meanwhile, the two policemen had handcuffed Colin and Ernie and were leading them to a police car.

'Why were they fighting?' I puzzled, mystified. 'And in the horse box of all places?'

'That's what I'd like to know,' said Jenny. 'It'll be very interesting to hear, but don't worry about that just now, twins. Put all your thoughts on the jumping.'

We reached the collecting ring just as the first pair of contestants were leaving after a clear round.

'Numbers eleven and twelve into the ring,' summoned the tannoy.

Desperately I tried to calm Cloud, who was trembling from her experience in the horse box. She crab-walked towards the entrance to the ring. She was still upset. What chance had we of completing a good round?

Pete was beside me as we went into the ring. 'Well this is it, Pippa. Stick with me.'

The bell clanged and we were off, heading for the first post-and-rails. Cloud gave a startled buck as I urged her to settle down. Pete and I cleared the post-and-rails together and set off for the road-closed.

So far so good!

We had to make a tight turn on the haunches, swinging our mounts round for the double. We jumped the first part well enough, but I felt Cloud put in an extra, nervous stride before the solid plank-fence that made up the second half of the double. Sure enough, she caught it with her near-hind and dislodged the lath.

'No clear round now,' I groaned to Pete as I tried to steady my mount for the hog's-back. It looked formidable because of its spread; yet it was quite an easy jump. We were over and away. Then, I know it sounds mad, but just at that vital point my thoughts strayed. I suddenly thought of Colin and Ernie! Why had they been fighting in the horse box? Had Ernie persuaded Colin to come to Boxheath especially to cut the ponies' plaits and why had the youths fallen out?

'Pippa!' Pete's voice was urgent at my side. Above the thunder of our ponies' hooves, he yelled: 'Down the middle, you chump! You're going off-course.'

15

Jump for joy

My confidence shaken, I pulled myself together as I realised that if Pete had not shouted I would have cantered round the outside of the course and set Cloud at the second double. We would have been disqualified for our mistake.

I swung the mare in too tight a turn. She responded willingly but slipped, half over-balanced, and nearly came down.

Meanwhile Pete had checked Cavalier. He was holding back his mount so that we would not incur a penalty by having too wide a gap between us.

The set-back had upset our timing. We approached the parallel bars too slowly and both ponies caught the second bar with their hind legs. The pole rattled and I glanced back to see it bounce in the cups and then fall.

Another four faults! Now we had eight in all!

'Do you think we should give up?' I called to Pete. 'We're just wasting everybody's time.'

'So what?' he grunted. 'Come on, Pippa. Carry on regardless.'

We cleared the gate and swung left-handed for the wall.

'Now then,' Pete urged from Cavalier. 'Give it all you've got. One, two, three, *up*!'

Miraculously we were over without touching the 'bricks'. The double lay ahead. The first part was composed of another pair of parallel bars. The second was a straight post-and-rails.

Cloud seemed to have got back her confidence. I felt purpose in her stride and left the timing to her. She jumped high over the parallel bars but not too wide, coming down beside Cavalier, with plenty of room to take off for the post-and-rails. We cleared the second obstacle and galloped for the finish—a single brushwood fence with narrow ditch on take-off.

Both ponies managed it easily. We reined up, trotted to the collecting ring and dismounted. We were about to lead our ponies back to the horse box when Jenny stopped us.

'Stay in the collecting ring,' she advised. 'You never know your luck. There may not be too many clear rounds.'

'Maybe,' I acknowledged, 'but there are sure to be two pairs who'll do better than our eight faults.'

Nevertheless we stayed beside Jenny to watch the fate of the other competitors. Number fifteen knocked down the second half of the double while his partner went on to take the next fence in the wrong order. He did what I had so nearly done,

continuing round the outside of the course instead
of turning up the middle, and so he was disqualified.

The next pair were girls riding their own ponies.
They had obviously put in a lot of practice together
and seemed unable to do anything wrong. They
took fence after fence and left the ring with a clear
round.

'That makes two clear rounds already,' Pete
groaned to Jenny. 'Pippa and I haven't a hope.'

When the next pair went into the ring, one of the
ponies napped. He spun round at the start, refused
three times at the first jump and was disqualified.
The next pair of competitors jumped well, but did
not keep together. In the end they had six penalties
for jumping separately, and another four for
knocking down part of the wall—ten faults, in all.

'Only one more pair to go,' announced Jenny,
and Pete and I watched anxiously as two boys,
obviously brothers, on well-matched greys rode into
the ring. Luck seemed with them from the start as
they cleared jump after jump, swung right down the
middle after the hog's-back, jumped neatly in and
out over the double and sped on to the parallel bars.
Here their luck seemed to change. The younger
boy's pony stumbled on take-off and crashed
through the jump, incurring four faults.

Glancing back, the elder waited for his brother to
catch up. They took the wall together but scattered
the bricks, knocked down the first part of the second
in-and-out and, losing hope, gave up without
tackling the last jump.

The judges awarded equal firsts to the two pairs with clear rounds.

'That means we're third.' I turned to Pete unable to believe our modest good fortune. 'We'll get rosettes after all!'

*   *   *   *

Yes, yellow rosettes—our first ever—adorned our mounts' head-bands when Pete and I returned to the horse box!

After unsaddling Cloud and Cavalier, we and Jenny were in time to join Sergeant Sam and the Colonel to watch Ian's dressage test.

When it came to Sultan's turn to enter the arena, the Arab shook his head a couple of times and gave a half-buck. The events of the morning had clearly unsettled Sultan and it seemed as though Ian would have a difficult time steadying the horse for a calm and disciplined performance.

'Number thirty-four—we're waiting,' repeated the tannoy. 'Number thirty-four into the arena, please.'

With an apparent calmness he must have been far from feeling, Ian rode Sultan in at a collected trot. Sitting down to the Arab's stride he looked right ahead. At the centre of the arena he halted, held the horse motionless for four seconds and then bowed to the judges.

'Sultan's not standing straight,' Jenny sighed. She turned to her grandfather as the Arab again tried to toss his head. 'I wonder if we'd have been wiser to scratch.'

Ian tightened his reins. Almost imperceptibly he shifted his weight from the Arab's quarters and began the rein-back. I held my breath as Sultan, keeping each step separate and deliberate, carried out the exercises.

'That's better,' muttered Pete.

Ian rode forward at the trot, dropped to a walk and then began the collected canter. With Ian sitting erect, Sultan rocking-horsed slowly around the arena.

It all looked so easy. Few people who hadn't seen it would have guessed at the Arab's panic flight from the fighting youths in the horse box earlier. Training showed as Sultan responded to Ian's every hidden aid, turning on his haunches, executing a flying change of legs, dropping from the canter to a working trot and then circling on either rein. The Arab seemed completely under Ian's control, yet I knew that beneath the facade of serene obedience, Sultan's nerves were raw from fright.

Now they were performing a counter-canter, outside legs leading, Sultan's head flexed inward over his leading foreleg and circling smoothly.

Then a vehicle leaving the car park backfired!

Sultan's ears flicked, his tail swished and twice he cantered on the spot. Losing his correct posture, Ian bent to pat the horse's neck. We saw him speak reassuringly to the Arab. As if nothing untoward had happened he carried on regardless to counter-canter in the opposite direction. He executed a sequence of collected and extended trots before walking down the middle of the arena, halting and bowing again to the judges.

When the scores were given out, Ian and Sultan were fifteenth, almost bottom of the list. 'He'll have to do exceptionally well in the cross-country if he's to stand a chance,' the Colonel sighed as we left the dressage arena and headed to take our places at the start of the course.

We could see only the first and last few fences although the Colonel's binoculars allowed him to report on another five. However, so far as we could judge, Ian was going well. When he came back into view, Sultan was galloping hard for the bank—the most feared obstacle of the course. We held our breath as the Arab jumped safely on to the top and leapt neatly over the pole. He negotiated the tricky descent by sliding half-way down the bank before jumping off. Then there was the zig-zag, a serpentine arrangement of post-and-rails which called for a good eye and expert timing on the part of horse and rider. Sultan jumped clear, flew the hay-rack and came to the coffin, a difficult obstacle with post-and-rails on either side of a sunken ha-ha—a hidden ditch.

As we watched, Sultan pricked his ears, and neatly jumped the post-and-rails. He seemed to size up the ditch, jumped high, but not too wide, and landed in time to take the second post-and-rails from a standstill.

'Well done, boy!' the Colonel exclaimed. He turned to Sergeant Sam. 'You've made a fine job of training that horse and his rider.' Pete and I exchanged glances. 'I only hope,' added the Colonel, 'that Major Rotherham, our inspector friend, is here to see how creditably your pupils are doing.'

Pete and I glowed as the Colonel's approving glance included us. It seemed as if the Colonel was definitely on Sam's side over keeping Stableways after all. We pressed forward to cheer as Ian and Sultan took the row of tyres—the final obstacle.

We hurried to pat Ian on the back and make much of Sultan as he dismounted.

'How was that for time?' Ian asked.

'Well within the penalty limit,' Jenny told him before her grandfather had a chance to speak. 'How did the jumping go?'

'Clear round, I think, and no refusals,' Ian said.

The voice over the loudspeaker confirmed that number thirty-four had a clear round and was first in the cross-country event so far.

While we were congratulating Ian, the tall figure of Major Rotherham joined the group.

'Well done,' he said to Ian and then turned to Sergeant Sam with a smile. 'I felt that I had to come across to congratulate you, Mr Harrington. I'm impressed by how well your pupils have done this morning in spite of all the difficulties.' He glanced towards the Colonel. 'Colonel Lyall has been telling me about the latest problems you've had to cope with. In my view you've done well, and now that the two hooligans have been caught, there should be no repetition of the trouble. I've already put in an interim report to the local authority saying that the situation at Stableways was under control. I shall now state that I consider the standard of safety and instruction to be satisfactory.'

'Thank you, Major.' Sergeant Sam almost stood to attention. 'We won't let you down.'

16

Something to celebrate

Yes, we felt we had something to celebrate that night, and so had the grown-ups.

The Colonel's housekeeper sent a buffet supper over to Stableways Cottage. Emma had been allowed to stay up late and was there with Rags, while Benny was wolfing all the food within reach.

'I don't think I can eat any more,' he told Sergeant Sam at last, with a half-eaten piece of pork-pie in his hand. 'Is it all right if I take this home for my dog?'

Jenny put on a record and soon the room seemed to be shaking as we all danced.

After a while Jenny withdrew from the fray. She winced as she touched her shoulder. 'My collar bone isn't yet up to all this,' she said. 'Why not give Pippa a turn Ian?'

Ian was fun to dance with, but all too soon the music changed to a slower, smoochy tune, and I felt a bit self-conscious dancing in the arms of an older boy who was so much taller than I was. Trying to appear cool, I congratulated him on his winning of the cross-country event.

'I made a mess of the dressage, though,' Ian said ruefully. 'All the same, it was amazing that Sultan did as well as he did after the turmoil in the horse box. 'Wait till I see that Colin! I'll give him a piece of my mind.'

Beyond Ian's shoulder I caught sight of two figures passing the window.

'You'll have your chance sooner than you think.' I told him in surprise as the door bell rang. 'He's at the door with Colonel Lyall right now!'

The beat quickened again, but the sitting-room door opened and Colonel Lyall came in, followed by Colin who was looking decidedly sheepish.

'Sorry to hold up the jollifications.' The Colonel signalled to Jenny to switch off the music. 'But this young fellow's got something to say to you all. He's already made a full statement to the police.' He pushed Colin forward. 'Carry on.'

Colin seemed tongue-tied for a moment, and then his words came in an embarrassed rush.

'I've been a complete idiot,' he told us. 'I thought I was helping my father because I knew he wanted to buy the Stableways land for building. Dad said that, if we could get Colonel Lyall to sell out and give Sergeant Sam notice to quit, we'd do up the house, live in it ourselves, and he'd buy me a couple of top-class show jumpers. I thought if I could make things go wrong at the stables the Colonel would be glad to sell—'

'And where did Ernie come into this?' Pete prompted as Colin momentarily dried up.

'I kept slipping him a few pounds and then Dad promised him double wages for looking after his vintage cars,' Colin said. 'But things got out of hand. Ernie was watching from the far end of the road last night when Colonel Lyall and Sergeant Sam arrived at his home to look for Rags. He did a U-turn on his motor-bike, came for me, and we decided to hole up in Brighton until things quietened down. But we didn't get far. Ernie had another rotten so-called brain-wave—to clip Sultan—and make him look such a freak that he wouldn't be able to compete at Boxheath.'

'Go on!' the Colonel prompted grimly.

'Well, after that I began to realise I didn't want to have any more part of Ernie's rotten tricks,' Colin told us. 'You may not believe this but that's really how I came to be fighting with him in the horse box. I'd had enough. Ernie had been boasting how he and a mate vandalised the practice jumps and put three of the ponies out of action while I was in hospital. This morning he didn't intend to stop at cutting out the ponies' plaits. He was going to hog their manes and shorten their tails. I had to prevent him. It wasn't easy because Sultan was panicking; that's why I let the Arab loose.'

'I suppose it's no use me saying I'm sorry.'

'Saying sorry isn't enough.' Sergeant Sam was stern-faced. 'Having a change of heart so late in the day doesn't wipe out what you did earlier. You went along with Ernie in terrorising the ponies. You condoned his putting the glass into Sultan's feed. It's not good enough.' He shook his head. 'You've got no backbone, lad. That's what's the matter with you. A lad with your advantages ought to have known better right from the start.'

In the uncomfortable silence that followed the Colonel escorted Colin out of the cottage. Emma ran after them, I suppose to hear more because a few moments later she came back, her eyes wide with scandal.

'Grandpa says Colin will be put on probation, and Ernie will be sent to a detention centre. Serve them right.' She called across to Jenny who was by the record player: 'Music, Jenny! Let's dance again. Grandpa says he definitely won't sell Stableways now. So it's Stableways for ever. Hip-hip-hurrah!'

END

Knight Books publish a wide range of fiction and non-fiction for boys and girls of all ages. If you have enjoyed this story, here are some more titles that you may like to read:

JUDITH BERRISFORD

PONY-TREKKERS, GO HOME!

The first book in the 'Pippa' pony series.

Pippa was overjoyed to be spending three weeks' holiday at her Aunt Carol's pony-trekking centre in Scotland. Even her brother Pete was converted when Lord Glencairn allowed the twins to ride his own expensive ponies.

But there was something that puzzled Pippa about Lord Glencairn's stables. Why were famous show jumpers lodged there – especially Ballantrae? And was there an explanation for the villagers' attitude towards the trekking centre?

Sworn to secrecy by Lord Glencairn himself, Pippa and Pete were left to try and solve the mystery themselves.

KNIGHT BOOKS

JUDITH BERRISFORD

A SHOW JUMPER IN THE FAMILY

The third story about the Brooke family and their ponies. Jane and Penny Brooke were discouraged when their father told them they weren't to show jump their ponies. Rusty, Penny's pony, had enormous potential and though the odds were all against her, Penny just *knew* she mustn't spoil his chances.

RUBY FERGUSON

The 'Jill' Books

JILL'S GYMKHANA
A STABLE FOR JILL
JILL HAS TWO PONIES
JILL ENJOYS HER PONIES
JILL'S RIDING CLUB
PONY JOBS FOR JILL
JILL AND THE PERFECT PONY
ROSETTES FOR JILL
JILL'S PONY TREK

KNIGHT BOOKS

JO FURMINGER

A PONY AT BLACKBIRD COTTAGE
BLACKBIRDS RIDE A MYSTERY TRAIL
BLACKBIRDS' PONY TREK

WALTER FARLEY

THE BLACK STALLION
THE BLACK STALLION RETURNS
SON OF THE BLACK STALLION
THE BLACK STALLION AND SATAN
THE BLACK STALLION'S FILLY
THE BLACK STALLION REVOLTS
THE BLACK STALLION'S COURAGE·
THE BLACK STALLION MYSTERY
THE BLACK STALLION AND FLAME
THE ISLAND STALLION
THE ISLAND STALLION'S FURY

KNIGHT BOOKS

JEAN RICHARDSON

THE FIRST STEP

The story of Moth Graham's first year at ballet school in London; her ups and downs, successes and failures, while adjusting to being away from home for the first time in her life. This book will strike an immediate chord with anyone who, like Moth, has longed to be able to dance.

DANCER IN THE WINGS

In her second year at *The Fortune School of Dance*, Moth is horrified to learn that the school's curriculum is being diversified to include lessons in acting and modern dance ... Sequel to *The First Step* this authentic picture of the worlds of pantomime and professional ballet will appeal to anyone who dreams of dancing.

KNIGHT BOOKS

MARY STEWART

A WALK IN WOLF WOOD

John and Margaret were picnicking in the Black Forest in Germany when, in the sleepy heat of the afternoon, an oddly-dressed man walked straight past them, weeping bitterly.

On impulse they followed him further into the forest, and that was the beginning of their adventure. Slipping back in time to the fourteenth century, the two children discovered a medieval world overlaid with the shadow of a dark magic, and only they had the key that could unlock the enchantment of the weeping man.

'Mary Stewart weaves her spell deftly, as ever.'
Daily Telegraph

By the same author:
LUDO AND THE STAR HORSE
THE LITTLE BROOMSTICK

KNIGHT BOOKS

MORE FICTION FROM KNIGHT BOOKS

☐ 26599 X   PONY-TREKKERS, GO
                 HOME!   85p

☐ 21657 3   A SHOW JUMPER IN THE
                 FAMILY   95p

☐ 24030 X   THE FIRST STEP   95p

☐ 26260 5   DANCER IN THE WINGS   95p

☐ 26537 X   A WALK IN WOLF WOOD   95p

All these books are available at your local bookshop or newsagent, or can be ordered direct from the publisher. Just tick the titles you want and fill in the form below.

Prices and availability subject to change without notice.

KNIGHT BOOKS, P.O. Box 11, Falmouth, Cornwall.

Please send cheque or postal order, and allow the following for postage and packing:

U.K. – 40p for one book, plus 18p for the second book, and 13p for each additional book ordered up to a £1.49 maximum.

B.F.P.O. and EIRE – 40p for the first book, plus 18p for the second book, and 13p per copy for the next 7 books, 7p per book thereafter.

OTHER OVERSEAS CUSTOMERS – 60p for the first book, plus 18p per copy for each additional book.

Name ....

Address...

....